THE LAST BLUES DANCE

Ferdinand Dennis was born in Kingston, Jamaica, grew up in London, and attended the University of Leicester and Birkbeck College (University of London). He has worked as a lecturer in Nigeria, a journalist and a broadcaster. His first book, *Behind the Frontlines: Journey into Afro-Britain*, won the 1988 Martin Luther King Memorial Prize. His first novel, *The Sleepless Summer*, enjoys a cult status in Britain's Afro-Caribbean community. He lives in London.

By the same author

FICTION
The Sleepless Summer

NON-FICTION
Behind the Frontlines: Journey into Afro-Britain
Back to Africa

FERDINAND DENNIS

The Last Blues Dance

HarperCollins*Publishers*

HarperCollins*Publishers*
77–85 Fulham Palace Road,
Hammersmith, London w6 8jb

A Paperback Original 1996
1 3 5 7 9 8 6 4 2

A catalogue record for this book
is available from the British Library

ISBN 0 00 649783 7

Set in Sabon by
Rowland Phototypesetting Ltd,
Bury St Edmunds, Suffolk

Printed and bound in Great Britain by
Caledonian International Book Manufacturing Ltd, Glasgow

For Dingle

The author gratefully acknowledges the financial assistance of the Authors' Foundation during the writing of this book.

Chapter One

From behind the window of the Caribbean Sunset Café
Boswell Anderson, grim and intense, watched Chatsworth
Road prepare for the rain. The passers-by hunched their
shoulders and hurried through premature twilight brought
on by a low sky of swirling dark clouds. A little way up
the street, two market stallholders who sold vegetables and
knick-knacks were unfurling the green canvases that would
protect them and their wares from the impending downpour.
Boswell's gaze drifted to the far side of the street, to the
Perpetual Beauty Hair Salon, where shadowy figures floated
behind a steam-covered window. Though it advertised itself
as specialising in West Indian and European hairstyles, its
customers were all black women. They had ignored the
weather and were having their recalcitrant hair pressed,
relaxed, jeri-curled, or braided with flowing extensions. Their
dedicated pursuit of eternal beauty had established the salon,
within months of its opening, as the most successful business
on Chatsworth Road. Boswell hoped that the rain would
end the drought of customers that had been afflicting his own
business for months. It was now mid-morning and only he and
Mona – the cook, who was in the kitchen reading a romance
magazine – had crossed the café's threshold since opening.

Somewhere in the east, towards Hackney Marshes, a drum
roll of thunder issued from the sky. Seconds later the rain
started. Despite the foreboding darkness and apocalyptic
rumbling, only a miserable drizzle fell. He remained at the
window until a fine mist enshrouded the street. The light
turned blue-grey: the city weeping.

Boswell turned and walked at a languid pace amongst the
crooked vinyl-covered tables and creaky chairs of his desolate
empire. Here he adjusted a chair, there he brushed a speck

of breadcrumb off a table. As he did so, he recalled the days when the Caribbean Sunset Café enjoyed a steady stream of loyal customers. During the day, laughter and conversation would fill the place and in the evenings the poker players came and stayed until early morning, leaving him with time for only a few hours' sleep, which was all he seemed to need. On weekend nights the basement walls would sweat copiously from the dancers who attended the blues dances there. Those days now seemed so distant that a haze of uncertainty overshadowed his recollections.

Noticing the brown stains, years of grease and nicotine, which discoloured the walls, he was invaded by a sense of futility. He felt obsolete, redundant, out of time and place; the feckless victim of ever-changing fashion, trampled on by the ineluctable march of history.

There was, indeed, something anachronistic about Boswell Anderson's appearance. He was a tall, lean man and wore a brown suit, the wide lapels and conservatively flared trousers of which suggested another era. His brown trilby hat, which he took off only at home, sat askew on his head, giving him a rakish appearance enhanced by bloodshot eyes which seemed to look on the world from some imponderable angle. He did not appear to be the sort of man who passed his days serving up tea and sandwiches and exchanging badinage with strangers, listening to their tales of woe and tribulation. Yet there was about him an indefinable aura, which intimated that he was somebody to whom the most horrendous secrets could be revealed without fear of disapprobation or disclosure, because he knew, had dwelt there for a lifetime, the dark murky regions of men's hearts.

He reminded himself of the plan he had implemented to revitalise the café, and his despair passed. For the past three months he had taken to playing poker again, ending a two-year retirement from the game that had once been his sole livelihood. He had spent four nights of every week in various minor illegal gambling joints. He had performed well and had accumulated a small sum of money. This past weekend had been particularly successful.

8

Boswell lit a cigarette and went to the counter. Resting on his elbows, his ankles crossed, he faced the street. Thus positioned he appeared to be relaxed, insouciant, like one waiting for an assignation in a strange place. He began sifting through the day's post, creating two piles: those inviting him to spend, and those reminding him what he owed. Both lots would end up in the bin; his funds were reserved for more important matters. Right now only legal threats would compel him to pay his bills. In his more contumacious days he had won a few court actions against these incessant nuisances and it crossed his mind to revive that practice.

The last letter quelled his rising bellicosity. It carried American stamps and a New York postmark. He had never received a letter from America before and had no idea he knew anybody in that part of the world. But he recognised the handwriting immediately. It was a letter from Cleo and he had been expecting it, with quiet patience, for three years.

Just then the Caribbean Sunset Café's door swung open. 'Bosy, Bosy Anderson,' a familiar but long unheard voice greeted him. It was Stone Mason, a bulky and impeccably dressed man. A cold blast of sorrowful air and a spray of rain accompanied his entry.

Boswell folded Cleo's letter with surreptitious haste, but neatly, and put it in his jacket pocket. He would read it later, in a quiet moment, as he had read all her letters over the past twelve years. What was Cleo doing in America?

'Stone Mason!' Boswell exclaimed. 'You're still alive, man! Is over a year I haven't seen you.'

Stone closed the door and moved to the counter with a celerity that belied his bulk and height. He was a towering figure with huge teeth and prominent bow legs. Stone Mason shook with the bass-filled laughter which was almost as renowned as his verbal halitosis.

'You lost your way?' Boswell said.

'Bloodclawt. No, mahn. Not at all. Is you me looking for and from what I see you're going to thank me one day.' Stone Mason gazed around the Caribbean Sunset Café and shook his head woefully. 'Things don't look so good, Bosy. Blood-clawt place could do with a coat of paint.'

'Don't tell me you've gone into interior decorating, Stone.'

'No. But imagine that I used to dream about owning a place like the Caribbean Sunset Café. There was a time when you were the centre of London. You used to bake a sweet potato pie that tasted like a Jamaican mountain morning after the rain. Remember those days when your blues dances attracted women more beautiful than a Caribbean sunset, and went on for days at a time? I hear you stop holding the blues dances, Bosy.'

'Ain't got the energy any more,' Boswell said.

'A bloodclawt shame. Met my wife in one of your blues dances.'

Boswell well remembered the romance between Stone Mason and Sandra Hoyte, the woman who became Stone's wife. They were just one of many couples who had met for the first time in the basement of the Caribbean Sunset Café.

'Glad to know you're still together,' Boswell said.

'And I hear you're back on the beat, playing poker again. Was told you wiped out those boys on Shacklewell Lane last weekend.'

'Didn't take much skill. Small stakes. I'm trying to raise the money to refurbish this place. Maybe turn it into a restaurant and takeaway joint. Put a bar in the basement.'

'That ambitious. Sounds bloodclawt good, though. When I heard you'd been playing with those rass amateurs I figured something was up. Mahn, you gone down in the world, Bosy. There's no money in those backwater houses. Look, I might be able to help you out, for old time sake.'

'You bring me some money?' Boswell laughed.

'Not quite, but almost. I've got a big game coming up. T-Bone Sterling is coming into town. He's a major poker player now. Owns two nightclubs in the Midlands. Drives a vintage Jaguar.'

'And he's playing at your place?'

'Yes, mahn. He's looking for a good game. Word is he's

going through a bad patch. Lose thousands of pounds. He's trying to play his way out of it.'

'A real gambler, eh?'

'He's good, mahn. Believe me. You want in? Can't give you an exact date yet. A month's time, three months. But I promise you forty-eight hours' notice, though. Usual house rules? Three days at the table.'

Despite his somewhat cool response to Stone Mason's invitation Boswell was quietly excited. He had been planning on playing in the minor gambling joints until he had amassed enough funds to secure a space at Stone Mason's far more lucrative table. Small fortunes had been won and lost there. Obviously word of his return had circulated faster than he expected. A good session against T-Bone Sterling could solve all his financial problems and help revive the Caribbean Sunset Café. He remained cool. With the skill of a man practised in the art of dissembling, he feigned a tepid interest.

'Give me a day to think about it,' Boswell said.

'Alright, but I must know by this time tomorrow. There's a whole heap of guys who'd sell their mothers to get in on this game. It's going to be big, mahn, bloodclawt big.'

When Stone Mason left, Boswell made a quick calculation. Various friends owed him over a thousand pounds. If he called in his debts and emptied his savings he would have a respectable stake.

An angry clap of thunder ended his deliberation. The downpour threatened all day by the menacing sky now started in earnest. Wind-driven rain lashed the window of the Caribbean Sunset Café, and streaks of lightning rent the sky, illuminating the café's aged interior.

The stampede of customers Boswell had earlier hoped for began with two middle-aged Caribbean women. Weighed down by their shopping, they entered gingerly and looked around with disapproving scowls, as if only an ill wind could have blown them to this fleapit – which was, of course, the case. Boswell instantly recognised in them ardent church-goers, hand-clapping, bible-thumping Pentecostalists. The sort of people who probably warned their errant children that unless they mended their ways they would end up in a place like the Caribbean Sunset Café. None the less Boswell assumed the mien of a humble servant and enjoined the ladies to rest their weary feet; they were under no obligation to buy even a cup of tea. His charm was irresistible. Soon the two ladies were ordering tea and fried dumpling and looking as if they daily dropped into the notorious Caribbean Sunset Café.

Comfortably seated, the women resumed a conversation which the rain must have interrupted. It seemed that one of their church sisters had been hospitalised with shock after a nocturnal encounter with a strange apparition, a figure in a grotesque elongated black wooden mask and shimmering gold ankle-length cape. She, the stricken woman, had wandered into Homerton Hospital, babbling and pulling at her hair. They had just visited her there. They agreed that their church sister had probably concocted this incredible story to conceal some shameful secret. After all, it was common knowledge that she was sweet on Rupert Harvey, one of the church elders.

Boswell eavesdropped on the women's gossip until the trickle of customers became a steady flow, demanding his full attention. Most of these customers, black and white, stayed only long enough to dry off and gather the courage to plunge back into the London rain, which always seemed to fall with vengeful fury over Hackney. Their meagre purchases did not dampen Boswell's optimism. The easy flow of his movements, the occasional repartee to blank-faced Mona, the dazzlingly endearing smile – all spoke of a man in his element. Fifteen years of running the Caribbean Sunset Café told him that this influx of customers was a heaven-sent opportunity and should not be wasted. Among these rain-soaked refugees were potential regulars. If they liked the atmosphere and the service, they would be back, foul or fair weather.

Hours later Boswell was still feeling optimistic, though the rain had ceased, and the Caribbean Sunset Café was nearly empty. Only two customers remained: Gilbert Singh, a Jamaican Indian and old regular who usually dropped in to pass the afternoon with Boswell, and Segun Adebayo, a quiet

Nigerian mini-cab driver who had recently started frequenting the café. When Boswell was alone Segun would talk to him, but on this wet afternoon he ate in pensive silence.

Mona had emerged from the kitchen. A short, stout young woman in her early twenties, she was ready to leave for home; a fact signalled by the too-large, misshapen blue overcoat she wore, and the shiny red plastic handbag she clasped to her chest like a little girl holding her favourite doll.

Boswell said: 'Not a bad day, Mona. Wait a while, eh? Segun will give you a ride when he's finished.' He was not in the habit of sending his employee home by cab but he felt generous towards the world.

'Sure,' Segun said, looking up from his meal and smiling.

Mona looked at him blankly, as if she had not understood. Without saying a word, she walked to the window, stood there for a moment, then took a seat. She reached into her handbag and brought out a magazine which had been folded and refolded so often to fit into her bag that, when spread out before her, it resembled a damp rag.

Boswell looked at Mona who was now engrossed in her reading, and shook his head pitifully. Having seen her with the same magazine for over a month, he had arrived, with some reluctance, at the conclusion that Mona was something of a simpleton. He now fully understood why his old friend Burt Xavier, Mona's father, had begged him to give her a job. Burt had hinted that she was less than normal. In the same breath he had mentioned that she was grieving for her late grandmother with whom she had lived in Dominica between the ages of five and twelve. Boswell could not say precisely what was wrong with Mona. Regarding her as simple was his way of coping with her peculiar behaviour. Yet he also appreciated her. She was the best chef and assistant he had ever employed. Once she was kept busy she performed her duties assiduously, which made her metamorphosis into this simpleton at the end of the working day all the more curious and disturbing. If only she paid more attention to her appearance, Boswell thought, she could be an attractive young woman.

When Segun and Mona were ready to leave, Gilbert Singh, who had been doing the crossword in the newspaper, decided he would go with them. 'I'll keep Mona's company for part of the journey,' Gilbert said.

'Mind that's all you do, or Burt Xavier won't be happy to know you been troubling his only girlchild,' Boswell said, laughing.

'You know me better than that, Bosy,' Gilbert said gravely.

'Well, Segun,' Boswell said, 'make sure you get this young lady home safe and dry now, or a lot of people won't have anybody to cook their lunch tomorrow.'

Segun's face lit up with a huge wide smile of perfect white teeth. 'Sure, sah, no problem,' he said.

Boswell handed him some coins for the fare and gave no more thought to Mona, Gilbert Singh or the young African. He locked away the day's takings, checked the kitchen and the back door, then turned out the lights. As he was locking the entrance to the Caribbean Sunset Café, another visitor arrived, Blake Matthews. Blake was a slow-speaking, lean youngster whom Boswell like to regard as the closest he had to a son. Years ago he had had a stormy relationship with Blake's mother, Carmen. As a result he had played surrogate father to twin boys who had only known their real father for brief periods in their childhood. Though the affair between Boswell and Carmen had ended in bitterness, Blake had remained attached to Boswell.

Blake stood about smoking a cigarette while Boswell finished locking up the café. Afterwards they walked up Chatsworth Road together like father and son.

'How's Barry?' Boswell asked. Barry, Blake's twin brother, had been in a mental hospital for the past year.

'Dunno. He's alright, I suppose, least that's what the doctors reckon.' His voice quivered with a subtle resentment, as if he objected to Boswell's innocent enquiry about his sick brother.

Boswell knew Blake well enough to sense when the young man was troubled. So he said nothing else and they continued walking in silence. Finally, Blake said: 'Why does everybody

14

ask about Barry? What about me? Nobody ask how I am, whether I am sick or anything. It's always Barry this, Barry that. I'm sick of it.'

They had reached a street corner where Boswell would turn for home. They stopped there, facing each other, two tall thin figures, one youthfully straight, the other with a slight stoop.

Boswell said with paternal severity: 'Told you a thousand and one times, Blake, get away from this neighbourhood, try another part of London. Better still, try another city or another country. Go and find yourself while you're young. To be lost in your youth is forgivable; to be still lost when your youth's done is a crime against yourself.'

Blake hung his head, as if in shame.

'You have money?' Boswell said.

'A few pounds.'

'Here,' Boswell thrust a ten-pound note at Blake, which he took gratefully. 'I know what's eating you up, Blake, we've talked about it enough. But you know there ain't nothing I can do about it. And right now, I am so tired. Check me tomorrow. We'll talk then. OK?'

'Sure, Bosy.' Blake walked away. When he had stepped off the pavement, he turned and said loudly to Boswell: 'Sorry, Bosy, and thanks. I'll see you tomorrow.'

Boswell continued his homeward journey alone, the usual jauntiness in his steps accentuated by a new mood of optimism induced by his acts of generosity and the surprise visit from Stone Mason. Things were looking up.

But passing the Church of Revelation and Redemption, he felt annoyed, almost belligerent. Elevated above the pavement, its neon-lit cross ablaze, its stained-glass windows brightened by the interior light, the church served to remind Boswell, as it did each time he passed it, of his enemy the Reverend Mordecai Morris. That fraudster, that cunning, low soul stealer. He cursed silently and hastened past the church. Once it was out of sight he recovered his equanimity.

Boswell's thoughts turned to his wife, Lorette, who had never been far from his mind throughout the day. They had been married for just over a year and he felt that he was still finding his feet in marriage. Of one thing he was certain, though: he loved Lorette dearly. He regretted that his recent and necessary return to the poker houses kept him out so late at night. Had Stone Mason not called at the café, Boswell would have probably gone out to play again tonight, returning after midnight. This was an improvement on his bachelor days but, he felt, hardly satisfactory for marriage. The promised session at Stone Mason's poker table now acquired a new importance. Not only would victory enable him to refurbish the café, transform the place into a new business, it would free him to spend more time with Lorette. So far she had shown extraordinary patience, and he was determined to reward her. He decided that he would buy her a gift tomorrow, something small and precious, like earrings or a brooch.

Stepping into his first-floor flat, Boswell was struck by a curious odour, at once sweet and rancid, like rotting fruits. He had smelt it before in the recent past, but never so arrestingly sharp and strong.

He hung up his hat and jacket, and went into the living room where Lorette was stretched out on the green mock Chesterfield sofa watching television. Seeing her banished all traces of the disturbing scent. She was dressed in a purple silk kimono which clung to the contours of her fleshy body and gave her a rather regal appearance. The skin of her broad, attractive face glowed with rude health and enhanced her somewhat otherworldly eyes. In Boswell's own eyes, she was a picture of well-preserved elegance, grace and beauty. His friends had often remarked that she had class and style. To imagine he had once suggested that she help him in the Caribbean Sunset Café!

She had laughed with playful scorn and said: 'You must be out of your mind.'

'Yes, for you,' he had said.

He had not mentioned the idea again, and now, after a day in that seedy café, it seemed like an absurdity of monstrous proportions.

He walked over to the settee, knelt beside her and said:

'Been thinking about you all day, baby; so I came home as early as I could.'

'Bosy, your tongue's sweeter than a field of sugar cane,' Lorette said, sucking her cheeks.

They hugged each other with forceful tenderness. In Lorette's embrace, her warm breath on his neck, Boswell felt as if his day had been a long, arduous journey, an ordeal; and this profoundly happy moment a priceless prize for successfully reaching the end.

After dinner Lorette, who had once been a professional singer, played the upright acoustic piano Boswell had given her as a wedding present, and sang. Hers was a pleasant, light voice with a plaintive resonance which infused even the happiest, most celebratory song with a subtle shade of haunting sadness. Boswell clapped vigorously through her performance, calling 'Encore!' when she sang a song he particularly liked.

There was, too, in Boswell's applause sincere gratitude for this beautiful woman who, in choosing to share his life, had ended a loneliness, always hidden behind his phlegmatic mask, which had persisted through, and contributed to the death of, innumerable affairs. Nevertheless, his attention was divided between Lorette and Stone Mason's invitation and its incalculable possibilities for the Caribbean Sunset Café.

Lorette was not insensitive to his distracted state of mind. Intermittently she paused and asked if he was bored. Would he prefer her to stop?

Boswell always said: 'No, no, play on, sing on.' He would listen for a few minutes before his thoughts strayed back to the café.

Later that night, with Lorette in the bathroom preparing for bed, Boswell again smelt the mysterious and disquieting odour, now fainter but no less palpable. He wandered into the bedroom and here the smell was stronger and brought to mind a fruit he had loved as a boy, but its name eluded him. He opened the bedroom window and cold damp air rushed in with the rattling metallic sound of a train on the line which ran beside the estate. The smell abated but a subtle trace remained, teasing and tormenting Boswell to name its source. Long after he and Lorette had retired Boswell was still awake. Sleep seemed as elusive as the end of a rainbow. He tossed and turned and got up several times to drink water in an effort to quench an unnatural thirst. Lorette slept soundly through his agitation.

All of a sudden Boswell thought he recognised the face of the disturbing scent. Nervously, he tapped Lorette's shoulder, and she murmured sleepily: 'What?'

In a choked whisper, Boswell said: 'You been sleeping with another man?'

'Don't be a fool, Bosy,' she said, turning round to embrace him.

He allowed her to hold him until sleep reclaimed her. Then he pulled away gently and lay on his back, stiff and cold like a corpse. Fearful for the dark days ahead, the dark days that would follow this night of anguish, this night suffused with the bitter scent of betrayed love.

Chapter Two

A burglary was in progress. Blake had used the money given him by Boswell to fill the tank of his car, a petrol-guzzling souped-up Mini which was mostly idle because he could ill afford to run it. Hours later he had driven to Highgate and broken into a house while its occupants were in bed. It had been a smooth entry, just as his informant – a telephone engineer called Tyrone, who had recently worked on the house – had promised. But easy beginnings can be deceptive.

Now, a door upstairs clicked open and a luminous path of light streaked under the door into the room Blake had violated. He instantly lowered his breathing and relaxed his muscles, entering a heightened state of alertness. He guessed from the sound of the weightless, hesitant steps brushing over the carpeted stairs that it was the woman of the house who was coming, coming softly. He would have preferred the man because he, Blake, the intruder, was young and strong and had an implacable confidence in his physical strength. He would have preferred the man because his crude armour contained nothing to stop the terrified scream of a woman.

He quickly reviewed his options: experience counselled him to take flight. A mixture of youthful pride and bravado challenged him to stay and hide in the hope that she would go away. He snatched up the gauntlet and dashed in swift silence to a place where he thought he would not be seen. This was a recess formed by a floor-to-ceiling mahogany shelving unit which contained the stereo, television, video and books. Deep and wide, it stopped short of a wall. The resultant alcove was occupied by a tripod-like table on top of which was a flourishing anthurium lily plant. He crouched and squeezed into a space there. Suddenly light flooded the room and the scent of jasmine impregnated the air. He heard her walk across the room to the window and close it, then back to the door. When the door clicked he thought it had been shut, and feared she had gone to telephone the police. His adrenalin pumped in anticipation of the flight ahead. He crawled from his hiding place, uncoiled and sprang towards the window. Through the side of his eyes he saw her pressed against the door. He stopped, and spun in a half-circle to face her. Their eyes locked. He now saw no option but to attack her, to buy time. He rushed towards her; and imagined he could already hear the shrill scream of this severe-looking woman with indecipherable gimlet eyes, could see the single accurate blow that would quieten her before his own frantic escape through the window.

Suddenly she raised an index finger to her lips and whispered: 'Shshshssh.' This sibilant sound, with its unexpected intimacy, arrested him for a crucial instant. He recovered but now advanced irresolutely, without any definite purpose, as if the scenario of brutal violence and desperate flight foreseen seconds before had been robbed of its appeal, its inevitability, its meaning. Then a thin nervous voice penetrated his confusion, and brought him to a sudden halt within inches of her face.

'My husband won't wake up,' she said through tremulous lips, 'if you don't make any noise. You can take what you want, but leave me something to remember your passing . . .'

Before the light dimmed he saw her lips twitch in a smile which even he, though now seized by an innocent bewilderment, recognised as a smile of desire. Soft hands stroked his face and neck, filling him with a curious passivity, a growing sense of detachment. Her warm dry lips pressed his mouth and her tongue, wet and blazing hot, followed, forcing his lips apart, snaking into his mouth. Involuntarily, he clasped her bony shoulders and returned her kiss with clumsy uncontrolled force. In the mixing of their juices he now felt himself journeying back from whatever far-off place of enthralment she had dispatched him. She pulled away and looked deep into his eyes, as if urging him across the final hurdle of conciliation with this great moment, this vital act. Then she crumpled gently to the floor of thick Persian carpet, pulling him down with her. He offered no resistance. Like a penitent before the cross of his salvation, he fell on his knees between splayed thighs incandescent in their whiteness. When she started to unbuckle his belt and unzip his pants with deft furtive movements his passivity passed. He finished unsheathing his tumescent rod and smothered her with his body. With a single violent thrust, he penetrated her desire. Between savage bites of his neck and ears, while her nails clawed at his naked buttocks, she commanded, exhorted and pleaded, 'Fuck me, fuck me until it hurts.' When he felt the pain of torn flesh and the warm trickle of blood where her fingers gripped him, he rammed into her in powerful motions, punished and rewarded her with a ferocious and merciless fury until she shook and shuddered in spasms of mounting urgency, until a powerful climatic explosion seemed to lift them both off the floor. Then he collapsed. Spent. Exhausted. Unbelieving.

He did not know how long he lay on the floor, locked in her arms. Now weary and confused, Blake crawled through the window, leaving the woman curled up on the carpet like a foetus. He had taken a gold inlaid tabletop lighter and a small silver statuette of a reclining nude nymph. He jumped from the window ledge into the garden, listened momentarily for a passing car or an approaching pedestrian. All was quiet; nobody was abroad on this tree-lined street at this late hour. He clambered over the garden wall, snagging his leather jacket on a rose bush and almost dropping his swag. He steadied himself and looked back at the house. He should have closed the window but it was too late now.

Suddenly he was aware that he was being watched. His gaze flew to the upper floor of the house he had just left. What he saw there, and saw with startling clarity, transfixed him for the second time that night: in the window, a pipe in his mouth, wearing a burgundy-coloured dressing gown over blue and white striped pyjamas, stood a grey-haired man. The man raised a hand, its palm seemingly luminous, and gave a gentle wave. He may have smiled, too. But Blake was neither sure nor interested. Seized by panic, he ran, fled with his confusion now a veritable storm.

Somehow he managed to find his car. But he did not drive away immediately. Instead he sat huddled up for a while, shaking feverishly as fragmented pictures of the burglary gone wrong replayed in his clouded mind. Unsure whether he had been violator or victim. Or both. The headlights of a passing car penetrated his consciousness. The smog of confusion and fear began to lift. He realised that he had hot goods on him; he had to get rid of them quickly.

He drove out of the quiet back streets onto Archway Road. Here, the constant stream of traffic helped to restore further a more balanced perspective on his situation. He tried to persuade himself that he was safe; the woman had wanted him; her husband had probably watched it all through the keyhole. But that burglary, the umpteenth in an erratic career of petty crime pursued less for gain than out of compulsion, would, he swore, be his last. It would be over once he got rid of the stolen things.

In Holloway, the disorientation he had earlier experienced returned with a feeling of nausea. He parked the car until he had regained his composure, then proceeded along Seven Sisters Road.

He stopped in Finsbury Park in front of what looked like a derelict house. The ground-floor windows were boarded up and blankets served as curtains over the top-floor windows. This was the home of Maddox, a fence who was rumoured to be a millionaire. Blake gave three rapid knocks, paused, then knocked rapidly twice more.

After a while a raspy voice said: 'Is who dat?'

Blake pressed close to the door and said: 'Something to sell.'

The door opened and Blake stepped quickly into a narrow, half-lit corridor. He stood before a small brown-skinned man with a straggly greying beard and tiny suspicious-looking eyes, like those of a rat. 'You know is almost two o'clock?' Maddox said querulously.

Blake knew that Maddox only slept a few hours each day,

and usually around early evening. 'You'll like this, man, nice and small.' Blake showed him the lighter and statuette.

Maddox snatched at them and Blake pulled them away playfully.

'Don't arse about or you can take them somewhere else,' Maddox said.

Blake handed over the swag and watched as Maddox expertly weighed them in his hands.

'OK, come upstairs.'

He followed the old man up the bare stairs into a dishevelled room at the back of the house. Maddox was more interested in the statuette than the lighter. He carried out a perfunctory test on the gold on the lighter, but scrutinised the statuette under a lamp, examining its base with a magnifying glass. It was a beautiful, tactile Victorian *objet d'art* which would be snapped up by a collector. He offered Blake, who had watched with impatient silence, fifty pounds for both items.

Blake protested and they bargained until Maddox made a final offer of seventy-five pounds, which Blake accepted, saying: 'I'm practically giving them to you. They're worth three or four times that.'

'OK, take them back,' Maddox said. 'Go and get two hundred pounds for them from somebody else.'

'Alright, alright,' Blake said.

From his back pocket Maddox took out a roll of soiled notes and counted out the agreed sum.

Back in the car Blake was invaded by a feeling of being cheated. Yet he knew that if he stole again, he would take the hot goods straight to Maddox because that crooked old man bought anything and everything brought to him. But as he drove further in to Hackney, towards home, the feeling that Maddox had short-changed him persisted and grew. Slowly a mood of generalised disaffection settled over him, and the woman who had seduced him and Maddox who had cheated him became indistinguishable.

He was now in Hackney proper. He turned left at the Lea Bridge Roundabout, then right onto Chatsworth Road and stopped outside the Caribbean Sunset Café. He knew it was closed but wished otherwise. So much had changed in such a short time, he thought ruefully. It seemed like only yesterday that whenever he tired of being Barry's shadow, he could wander aimlessly at night and end up in Boswell's company. Sitting in the blue-lit basement, with Boswell sipping Scotch, and melancholy old reggae music playing on the stereo, he would feel secure and contented. Maybe Boswell would talk about the season he picked oranges in Florida, the great poker games he had played, the women he had loved and lost. Maybe the proprietor of the Caribbean Sunset Café would lecture him about the eternal sorrow that is life, and the need to seize those rare, brief moments of happiness, which only a man who knew himself could recognise. Blake looked at the café's darkened window and imagined he heard Boswell saying, as he did on many occasions: 'Go home and sleep. Whatever monster's troubling you mightn't seem so terrible in the morning.'

He was trying to stir himself to turn the ignition key when he saw a bizarre figure approaching. It staggered up the road, reeling from the edge of the pavement to the shop windows, struggling with its elongated head as if trying to remove it. Fear seized Blake and, in an effort to hide, he slid lower in the car seat. As the creature neared, Blake could make it out more clearly. The chin of its long, angular face reached down to its chest and its high tall forehead climaxed not in hair but in a crown of minute figures which, as the streetlights played on them, seemed all at once to be writhing in agony, laughing and dancing. The body was covered in what seemed like golden straw, arranged in the style of a cape. The figure stumbled past, a gleaming mass of black and gold, a fabulous and frightening spectre.

Blake followed its progress in the car's rear-view mirror until it turned into a side street. Then, fumblingly, he started the car, and raced away towards home, fearing that the apparition was yet another sign of his weakening grip on reality.

Blake's girlfriend, Sheila, was asleep when he reached home, a single-bedroom flat on the fourteenth floor of

Worthington House, which overlooked Hackney Marshes. He went straight to the bathroom. He undressed and saw with giddy horror bloodstains on his T-shirt and underpants. He wanted to bathe but, worried that the noise would wake Sheila, arouse her suspicion, he settled for changing his underclothes in the dark. Then he climbed into bed beside Sheila, who rolled over to the far side, as if repulsed by his presence.

'Your mom called by this evening,' she said sleepily.

'What did she want?'

'To remind you about going to see Barry next week.'

'Bloody hell, she knows she doesn't have to do that.'

There was no reply and Sheila began to snore gently. Blake lay on his back unable to sleep, a swarm of thoughts buzzing in his mind. Slowly they began to separate. He would have to give some money to his friend Tyrone, but there wasn't much to give; he anticipated an argument. He wondered about Barry again and wished that the body lying next to him was that of his brother. He could talk about how he felt used and dirtied by the woman and Maddox, could reveal that he had seen a monster, a ghost stumbling along the street and how it had terrified him. Barry would have probably laughed pitilessly, but that laughter would have cleansed him, purged him of his anxieties. God, I miss you, Barry, he thought: if you hadn't fallen ill I'm sure I wouldn't have gone back to burglary, no matter how many easy chances came my way. If you were here I wouldn't feel so cold and alone and scared.

He fell asleep thinking of his mother.

Chapter Three

In that hazy moment between waking and rising, when receding memories of dreams seem like memories of real events, and reality seems like a new dream unfolding, Boswell could only smell Lorette's sleepy body mixed with a trace of her night perfume. The usual innocent scents of mornings that followed a physically passionless night. As he lay there wondering whether it, the odour of betrayed love, had all been a dream, Lorette stirred. And in the somnolent voice with which she made the same request every morning, she asked for a parting hug. He obliged dutifully but half-heartedly, but she held him with such desperate tenderness, such reassuring affection, that, to Boswell, his failure to reciprocate seemed cruel. Slowly, his torturous night now began to appear like the nightmare of a man afraid of losing the most precious thing in his life. He remembered how, in the first months of courting Lorette, insecurity so plagued him that each time they parted he feared he would never see her again, because all his adventures in love had ended disastrously. Locked in Lorette's arms after that night stained with the scent of betrayed love, he remembered the awesome power of dreams to unearth a man's worst fears. So he held her properly now, clasped her to his pulsating heart which overflowed with bountiful gratitude for the realisation that it was only fear that had poisoned his night.

She murmured, 'What an awful night. Had all kinds of strange dreams but I can't remember them.'

'Me too,' Boswell whispered, kneading her coccyx, a spot he knew she liked massaged. Her skin had never felt softer to his fingers, her sleep-laden breath on his face sweeter, her love so strong. She rolled on top of him and Boswell, almost tearful with joy, did not care if the Caribbean Sunset Café opened late that morning.

By the time he reached the café, Boswell had resolved to cast aside his foolish suspicion, put the episode out of his mind. Another empty morning would have weakened this resolve, caused him to brood on his fear of losing Lorette, but fortunately the rain resumed with the working day, bringing in a steady flow of damp customers on whom Boswell – now the sympathetic listener, now the raconteur, now the complaisant waiter – bestowed his apparently undivided attention. When he thought of Lorette, he thought of the glorious reward awaiting him at the day's end.

He did manage to snatch a few minutes from this happily busy day to telephone Stone Mason and confirm his participation in the poker game with T-Bone Sterling, when it happened. Stone Mason was delighted. Boswell had to hold the telephone away from his ear, such was the torrent of swearwords from his friend.

But the furious rhythm of the day conspired against him finding the peaceful moment he needed to read Cleo's letter. The next day he changed his suit, and Cleo's letter, forgotten, still in his pocket, was sent to the dry-cleaner's. Until he rediscovered the letter, Boswell would occasionally pause in the middle of a task and try to remember something he should have done, yesterday or the day before. But in the busiest week the Caribbean Sunset Café had known for years the existence of the unread letter from his former lover was completely overlooked.

The weekend came, and if they had not had a prior engagement to attend the farewell party of Bobby and Marion Summers, who were returning to Jamaica after thirty years in London, Boswell and Lorette would have spent it in bed. But duty was duty. So on Saturday night they deigned to go out into the world.

They almost didn't make it beyond the bedroom. Boswell, whose wardrobe was somewhat limited, had donned his best brown suit, and was heading for a drink to occupy himself while Lorette dressed. But she detained him in the bedroom by seeking his advice on which of two outfits she should wear. Boswell made his choice, then lingered by the door as she sat on the edge of the bed and began slowly to pull black tights over shimmering, shapely legs, which, like the rest of her body, were a dark reddish brown colour. He had seen her dressing on many occasions but he had never really watched. Now he noticed the methodical slowness with which she prepared herself; how she scrutinised her reflected body from head to toe, from front to side, to back; how she pinched and squeezed the rolls of fat around her midriff and scowled disapprovingly. Each gesture seemed to bury her deeper into this critical self-admiration. Boswell felt as though he were a stranger watching a deeply personal ritual. Desire stirred inside him. Bobby Summers' farewell party could wait, he decided, approaching her. She started, as though he had caught her unawares and shattered the moment of privacy. She laughed embarrassedly when he suggested that they dally a while, but did not resist his caress.

After they had showered, Lorette chased him out of the bedroom. When she reappeared Boswell was stunned. Lorette was wearing a plain, finely woven body-hugging black woollen dress, complemented by a fan-tailed, cream-coloured linen jacket with gold stitching. It was not the outfit he had chosen. But her jewellery – oval-shaped earrings of silver and malachite and a matching brooch, his present to her – appeased any annoyance he felt at his choice being ignored. Two grey streaks in her lightly permed hair, a narrow one running down the centre of her head, a broader band above her left ear, contrasted with her still youthful figure and face. For Boswell, she was a woman who had transmuted the ravages of time – without resort to the illusory disguise of heavy cosmetics; she wore only eyeshadow and lip gloss – into simple adornments. Without them she would be beautiful still; with them her beauty acquired subtle qualities of mystery and grace.

Boswell fell in love with his wife a second time that night. Only Lorette's reminder that he was supposed to speak at the party prevented him from delaying their departure yet again.

The valedictory party for Bobby and Marion Summers was held at a community centre near Hackney Downs. The occasion had flushed out an army of old friends and acquaintances whom Boswell had not seen in years. Men and women who used to frequent the Caribbean Sunset Café in its halcyon days. They had drifted away, claimed by the routines of ordinary domesticity, marriage and parenthood. Now and again he had seen them hurrying along Stoke Newington High Street or shopping in Ridley Road market. The women with resentful-looking children trailing behind them as they inspected the plantains and yams and sweet potatoes they were considering buying. The men tired and fretful, their faces etched with the lines of family responsibilities and burdens, their brief exchanges with him hinting that he belonged to a past they had left behind, irrevocably, thankfully. He had not seen them again in the Caribbean Sunset Café.

Somehow Boswell got separated from Lorette by these old-timers. They all seemed curious to find out what Boswell had been up to in the intervening years, whether he still ran the café. Boswell gradually became aware of who was there as much as who was not there. Dixie Peters, whom Boswell had allowed to sleep in the Caribbean Sunset Café while searching for a room, told him about attending Buzz Campbell's funeral. It had been a quiet subdued affair attended by a handful of mourners, who had not been especially close to the deceased. Buzz Campbell had died of loneliness in an unheated Finsbury Park bedsit six months after his wife decided that she could not face another London winter, could not wait for the end of the five years that she and Buzz had originally agreed to spend in England. The half-built house – windowless, doorless – in St Thomas, which represented their life's savings and dream, with its view of the blue, blue Caribbean Sea, would suffice for her. So she had left Buzz here and he had promised to join her in a year's time. But he had not made it. Instead his life had turned ice blue with death.

Before Boswell had fully digested Dixie Peters' tragic tale, another of the men, Frank Bailey, with whom he stood, said:

'You know when I first came to England that was my biggest fear, dying in some cold, lonely room. But last year I bought a house in Kingston. Plenty land around it. Plenty fruit trees, mango soursops. And a lovely pear tree; you know the one that bears them big purple pears. Lovely. That's where I'll die.'

Yet another man, Carlton Ricketts, said: 'It's the country for me. Got a cosy little cottage in Clarendon. The verandah's got a view of the hills and peace is all around.'

'By the way, Bosy,' Frank Bailey said, 'I ran into Lance Tomlinson, Rupert Phillips and Cuthbert Harrison last time I was in Kingston. They're all real Kingstonians now. Anyway, Tomlinson asked when you're coming home, Bosy; whether you're waiting for the Englishman to repatriate you?'

They all laughed good-heartedly, including Boswell, who simultaneously glanced around for Lorette. She was engrossed in conversation with a group of ladies. Boswell longed to be reunited with her. But his acquaintances detained him further when Frank Bailey said: 'But you know is true, Bosy. I've known you for over twenty years and I've heard you talk about home but never actually going home.'

This remark heightened Boswell's eagerness to escape from these men, with their discomforting talk of death and departure. He saw in the proud lined faces of those around him the contentment of men who had lived out most of their simple ambitions and now had one remaining: to live a good death. A spasm of sadness shook him, and he thought: So many people I knew have gone home or are going home. How could he tell these men that he was different from them; that he had always been different because he had never had a vision of a home to which he would one day return?

After a seemingly long pause, Boswell said: 'Home? Man, I'm like the spider. I carry my home on my back and spin my web in any dark warm corner, like Hackney, to make a home.'

'That's true,' Dixie Peters said. 'I could go away for twenty years and come back to find Bosy still running the Caribbean Sunset Café.'

They laughed again and with their laughter the apparent mystery of why Boswell did not talk about going home vanished. When Carlton Ricketts began talking about a friend who claimed to have seen a strange, disturbing figure late one night on Hackney Downs, Boswell seized the opportunity to escape. He went to join Lorette, whose own circle had thinned out. Reunited with her, he held her hand until the PA system cackled to life. The speeches were about to begin.

The first speaker, a former mayor of the borough, almost ruined the evening with a tedious and lengthy peroration. The spacious community hall in which they stood had been built during his tenure. His entire speech praised his own heroic role in helping to end the days when the only meeting places for West Indians were damp basement venues run by dubious characters. His very last sentence casually wished Bobby and Marion Summers, who stood beside him, a happy return to the Caribbean.

The next speaker was more focused, but almost as long-winded. The MC next called Boswell, introducing him as a pioneering black entrepreneur. Sensing the crowd's restlessness, Boswell was determined to make a short speech. Leaving Lorette at the side of the hall, he made his way to the front and took the microphone. Unfortunately, the PA system went awry with his first words and he had to stop. While two men worked to fix it, Boswell scanned over the pool of heads for Lorette. At first he could not see her, but he continued looking. Then he saw her smiling and patting her hair and talking to a stranger. The man hovered disturbingly close to her, the closeness of a man with unmistakable predatory designs. She was clearly enjoying his attention. Jealousy flared in Boswell, like the eruption of a volcano. He wanted to abandon the microphone immediately and intercede. He saw her laugh a coy laugh which he remembered from their first encounter. Suddenly, the microphone cackled back to life. For a fleeting second a distracted Boswell held the instrument as if uncertain of its purpose. It was Bobby Summers' cough which snapped him out of the hypnotic daze caused by witnessing a man sweet-talking his wife. He started, determined to make his speech even shorter.

'Ladies and gentlemen,' Boswell said, desperately trying to keep his eyes focused on the centre of the hall, rather than the side where Lorette was. 'Ladies and gentlemen, I've known Bobby Summers for nearly twenty-five years. There was a time, long ago, when me and Bobby were two lonely men, scouring these streets of London that were then strange and hostile, looking for our fortune, looking even for love. When Bobby met Marion in the Caribbean Sunset Café, he found love, and I encouraged their romance and marriage, though Bobby didn't think he was good enough for Marion. I'm happy to know that Bobby has also found the fortune that eluded us both years ago. Now I know why I haven't seen Bobby or Marion in the Caribbean Sunset Café for years. They've been saving up for the great day when they can see a real Caribbean sunset for ever and ever.

'Bobby and Marion, we will miss you. But we will always remember you both with warmth and joy. And as you sit on your verandah in the evenings watching the sunset over the Caribbean, remember those of us you left behind.

'A toast to Bobby and Marion Summers, and safe passage home, to their eternal happiness.'

Boswell raised his glass and the crowd followed, cheering and clapping tumultuously. Before the applause subsided, he handed the microphone to the MC and began making his way through the hall towards the place where he had last seen Lorette. But his progress was hampered by several appreciative guests who stopped and congratulated him for the exemplary brevity of his speech and the accuracy of its sentiments. These delays heightened his anxiety to get to Lorette. Who the hell is that man? was a question that resounded in his mind even as he accepted the compliments.

When Boswell, trembling with jealousy, finally reached the spot where he had left Lorette, where he had seen her basking in a strange man's attention, he found only the ghost of her absence.

Chapter Four

Segun Adebayo was thinking about Sade as he slipped the
battered Rover down into second gear, roared past a BMW
of blinding newness, swung left at Shoreditch and headed
north, along Kingsland Road, towards Dalston. He had
dropped a passenger at Liverpool Street station, his last in
three consecutive days of working. He was tired and his longing for Sade was sharp and deep and painful; it throbbed
inside him like a cancerous tumour. He had looked for her
in Lagos. He had looked for her in Liverpool. Now he was
looking for her in London. She was somewhere in this teeming
ancient city. He could feel her presence. When he found her,
however many weeks, months or years it took, when he found
Sade he would fall to his knees in supplication and beg her
to come back. O, Yemanja, goddess of the sea, give me
strength and endurance, he prayed silently. O, Yemanja,
wise and beautiful goddess, daughter of the Supreme Being
Omodumare, lover of Ogun, god of travellers, mother of
Oshun, goddess of the river; O, Yemanja, bless my quest,
guide and protect me in this strange city, so that I may find
my love, the flame of my heart, my sole reason for living.

The mid-morning traffic slowed to a crawling pace near
the Geffrye Museum, a low green building arranged around
a grassy front which interrupted the monochrome of this
thoroughfare. The mini-cab driver was too exhausted to trawl
his memory for an alternative route through the labyrinthine
backstreets. Besides, he did not have to report to the office
until midnight; and even at this speed he would easily keep his
appointment in Stamford Hill, to view a room. This prospect
cheered him somewhat: a space of his own in London after
six weeks of sharing a poky, overcrowded garret with three
of his compatriots. If he liked the room, and the landlord

liked him, he would move in straight away. Maybe I'll drop into the Caribbean Sunset Café for breakfast, he thought; there's plenty of time.

The traffic came to a halt and, finding himself falling asleep, Segun Adebayo switched on the radio. It cackled to life and a coarse, angry voice chanted: 'Nuff respect to all de Hackney posse, nuff respect to all de listeners, nuff, nuff, nuff respect to all de ravers, nuff, nuff respect. Tonight I want all you members of de Hackney posse to head right down to that wicked, wicked Nations nightclub tonight and Big it up, Big up you'self inna dance-hall stylee.'

Segun turned the dial to find some soothing station. Everybody in this city was angry, he thought, the passengers he carried daily, his boss at the cab office, the people on the streets. They all wore their anger like medals of war. He looked forward to the day when he found Sade and returned with her to Lagos. There at least, despite all its shortcomings, people still had the gift of laughter.

The vehicles in front started moving again and continued at a slow pace until they reached Dalston Junction. Stuck at the traffic lights, Segun scrutinised the young women on the crowded sidewalk. But there was no sign of Sade amongst the angry, glum-painted faces, no sign of her dark bright eyes, her enchanting smile.

A car horn blew; the lights had turned green; he turned into Dalston Lane, his eyes still searching the faces. He drove to Homerton and parked his car a block from the Caribbean Sunset Café. He would have breakfast there, he decided, rubbing the sleep from his eyes as he walked.

The café was empty but for the proprietor, Boswell Anderson, who sat behind the counter, his face resting in his hands, a ruminative glaze in his eyes. Eventually he said: 'Ah, my Nigerian friend and favourite customer, welcome.'

Segun, on discovering the Caribbean Sunset Café, had returned again and again solely because of the warmth of Boswell's greeting. The proprietor had an uncanny ability to put him at ease. In one of his early visits to the café, Boswell had quipped that he, Segun, 'looked like a youngman in

34

search of something lost.' The accuracy of this remark had endeared Boswell to him too, though he had not told him about Sade.

He ordered a large breakfast of eggs and toast and coffee, and took a seat near the window. He ate it in silence. When he had finished he realised he still had over an hour to kill, so when Boswell came to take his plate away, he delayed him in small talk.

'That was delicious,' Segun said.

'Thanks, I'll tell Mona. Maybe your compliment will bring out one of her rare smiles. She doesn't do it often but when she does it's as beautiful as a Caribbean sunset.'

'The food is so good here. I don't understand why you don't get more customers, Bosy.' Segun glanced around at the empty chairs and tables.

'Wasn't always like this, you know,' Boswell said. 'There was a time when this place was busier than Waterloo station.'

'What happened?'

'Oh, times change,' Boswell said.

Segun noticed Boswell's sudden rueful expression. The proprietor now sat down opposite Segun, as if his question had been an invite to take a seat. He welcomed Boswell's presence.

'It's more than that, though,' said Boswell. 'Much more. I lost most of my customers because of a godman.'

'A godman!'

'Yes, a preacher. You know the Church of Revelation and Redemption? The one with the neon cross?'

Segun nodded.

'Well, the man behind that, the Reverend Mordecai Morris, drove away my customers,' Boswell said bitterly. 'See, I used to hold blues dances here, in the basement. People came from far and wide for the blues dance at the Caribbean Sunset Café. Now, the Reverend Mordecai Morris, he was just plain Mordecai Morris when he first turned up here, asking to rent the basement for three hours every Sunday afternoon. Practically went down on his knees and begged me. See, in those days we, black people, didn't have many spaces to gather in. Not like today. Anyway, eventually I agreed. Used to spend Sunday morning cleaning up the basement, washing away the spirit of Bacchus, to prepare it for holy worship. Kept that up for about three months.'

Segun noticed the pride and hurt in Boswell's voice. From the kitchen came the clanging sound of a dropped pot lid. Boswell lit a cigarette, glanced round the café, and continued.

'But one Sunday morning, it was like people just didn't want to go home. The blues just went on and on. The morning passed like the passing of a timid man. Nobody took any notice. The Reverend Mordecai Morris turned up with some members of his small flock to find bodies entwined in all sorts of lewd dances, the air sweet with all sorts of forbidden pleasures. I didn't see him again for a while. But when I next saw him, I regretted ever having set eyes on that man. Him and his flock were gathered outside the café, singing hymns. And between these hymns the man was likening the Caribbean Sunset Café to Sodom and Gomorrah, and me, Boswell Anderson, me who had given him a meeting place, to an emissary of the devil. They kept that up for months. Would swoop on us at all kinds of funny hours. Late at night, early morning.

'Well, I can't say I had the best class of customers. Married men with their girlfriends, pimps with their prostitutes, gamblers. Lost a few gamblers to him. They became his most rabid disciples. The others, people who needed somewhere quiet to conduct their businesses, just started drifting away. Things have never been the same since. I'm not a man who has enemies. But that Reverend Mordecai Morris, to this day, is my most hated enemy.

'I hope you're not a godman,' Boswell said, suddenly laughing.

This mercurial switch from what was clearly an embittered recollection to laughter made Segun even fonder of Boswell.

'No,' Segun said. 'I have gods, and they're personal gods. I would not use my belief to persecute another man.'

'I knew there was a reason I liked you instantly,' Boswell said, laughing again. He took Segun's plate and cup, stood up and said: 'One day, I'll tell you how I stopped the Reverend

Mordecai Morris's campaign. Wasn't a nice thing I did. But I had to do it.'

Segun was tempted to ask Boswell to tell him there and then, but noticing the time, he decided he had better set off for his appointment. Paying for his breakfast, he sensed that Boswell's mood had changed yet again. He now wore a lugubrious expression, as if saddened by his memories. Yet when Segun bade him goodbye, he switched again to that cheerful, happy-go-lucky persona that he normally showed. Which is the real Bosy? Segun wondered as he stepped out of the Caribbean Sunset Café.

The café and its proprietor were far from his mind when he reached Stamford Hill. He found the street and house without any difficulty. The house was indistinguishable from all the other redbrick terraced houses which lined the street. It gave no sign that it would be his new home. He was early and, as he waited, he noticed a number of bearded men in long, dark coats, and hats, with ringlets of hair hanging from their temples, framing their faces. The male children were smaller versions of the adults and had the same silent, studious, ancient air. Somebody had told him that they were Hasidic Jews, a people who had clung to their traditional ways over many centuries and continents. He regarded them with curiosity and admiration, and felt more kindly towards London because it could accommodate such a variety of peoples.

At the appointed hour Segun rang the doorbell. Nobody answered so he sat and waited on the portico wall. He had been there for a while, drifting in and out of sleep, when a voice woke him.

'Come to see about the room?' The man who had addressed him was white, with a craggy, clean-shaven face. He was balding but his hair seemed to have been arranged with precision to disguise it. His thick fingers were laden with gold signet rings, and his clothes – navy-blue Crombie, shiny black shoes, shiny grey suit and a black turtle-neck jumper – suggested a man going out for a night at the pub, rather than a landlord. His eyes had the shiftiness of a man with many enemies. But Segun did not notice this. He was still new to London and had not yet learnt to read the people, especially the white folks.

'Yes,' Segun replied. 'If it's still going.'

'Sure is,' the man said, his jaws working a piece of chewing gum. He opened the door with a thick bunch of keys and they entered a hallway.

'Nice room, you'll like it,' he said, and they climbed the stairs to the first floor.

The room was indeed nice. It needed a fresh coat of paint and the bed, sunken in the middle, looked as if an elephant had slept in it for a year. A large window gave a view over a long garden cluttered with discarded furniture but with plenty of trees and shrubs. The neighbouring gardens were well tended. Segun liked it instantly. With some pictures of his own and some more furniture it would make a wonderful temporary home for him and Sade, when he found her.

'And it's a bargain,' the fellow said. 'Fifty-five pounds a week, and four weeks' rent deposit and four weeks' in advance.'

The Lagosian in Segun could not resist the temptation to bargain. 'I'm a poor student, working my way through college. Couldn't you make it forty-five pounds weekly and take just a month's deposit?'

The man grinned and said, 'Company policy, the deposit and advance. I can't change that.'

'How about the rent?'

'OK, these are hard times. I'll give it to you for fifty quid a week, and we'll review the rent in three months' time.'

That was exactly the figure Segun had in mind. He accepted instantly. 'How soon can I move in?'

'Soon as you give me the deposit and advance, sunshine, it's yours.'

Excited by the prospect of having his own room, Segun threw caution to the wind. He went to his car, opened the boot, and from under the spare wheel took four hundred pounds from his savings of five hundred. He would, he decided, collect his things from his shared room later that day.

Segun signed a form which the man had presented to him. Money and keys were exchanged in a smooth transaction and there was much shaking of hands and laughter.

Segun drove straight away to Homerton and gathered his few belongings from the attic room, while one of his erstwhile flatmates, who worked the nightshift in a canning factory, snored loudly.

Then he drove back to Stamford Hill. He now noticed how much wider the streets were here, how much larger the houses – altogether he was in a better part of town. Sade would be proud of him. Weighed down with the plastic bags of all his worldly possessions, he approached the door of his new home-to-be. As he put the key in the lock he wondered who the other tenants were, whether they might be able to help him find Sade. His first attempt to open the door failed; the key fitted the lock but he was unable to turn it. He tried repeatedly and with each effort his frustration mounted. Then he knocked on the door, gently at first; then increasingly hard.

Frustrated but hoping that the man had mistakenly given him the wrong keys, he found the rental contract. The number on it corresponded with the number which he had called to enquire about the room. He drove to a phonebox on Stamford Hill and dialled. After a moment of silence, a toneless recorded female voice said: 'The number you are calling is no longer available.' He listened to it again before its full meaning sunk in: 'The number you are calling is no longer available.'

Chapter Five

It was the end of another unprofitable working day and Boswell was alone in the Caribbean Sunset Café. Since the night of Bobby and Marion Summers' farewell party, he had been in the grip of a melancholy born of love and the fear of losing love, bittersweet like fermented guava juice, as bitingly sharp as green oranges. Lorette's behaviour there had revived his suspicions. He had searched for her, with his imagination running amok. When he had found her she told him that she had gone to the ladies' room and the long queue there had delayed her return. So she had said. He had forcefully insisted that they leave immediately, almost causing a scene. On the way home he had accused her of inviting and revelling in the attention of a stranger. She had laughed and said: 'Every woman likes attention, Bosy.' This facetious, though honest, reply had not amused Boswell. Indeed, it exacerbated his jealousy and deepened his fear. And since that night he now daily smelt the cloying odour of betrayed love when he arrived home. But what could he do? He had no proof.

Earlier that day too he had left Mona in charge of the café and gone home in the fearful hope of catching Lorette in the act. He had found her alone, playing the piano and singing Gershwin's 'Summertime' at a slow pace, like a dirge. How beautiful she had seemed then, her back straight, her long fingers dancing gently on the keyboard. He had made a feeble excuse for his unexpected presence, rooted around the flat, ostensibly searching for some document, and departed with that infuriating scent lingering in his senses.

When the café door swung open and Bobby Summers and Frank Bailey came rolling in, singing, 'Carry me ackee go a Linstead Market', Boswell again regretted having attended that wretched party. The two men had been drinking and each held a bottle of rum. Boswell rearranged his face and greeted his two intrusive visitors as if he had been waiting for them all day. These buggers must be chasing me, Boswell thought, taking out three glasses, resigning himself to their garrulous, inebriated company.

After a shot of rum Boswell surrendered himself to the spirit of the evening. And it turned out to be profitable. He received a cheque for two hundred pounds from Bobby Summers. It seemed that years ago, in the earliest days of the Caribbean Sunset Café, Boswell had loaned Bobby a small sum of money, which Bobby had gambled on a horse. He had invested the winnings, which had grown to a handsome size, and, as part of his preparation for leaving England, he was settling all his debts. When the visitors were leaving, Bobby Summers glanced around the café, frowned and said: 'Mahn, Bosy, is a mystery to me why you want to stay in this country. If I owned this place, I'd sell it and go home.'

Boswell disguised his unease at Bobby Summers' advice with loud laughter and bade his visitors farewell. When they'd gone, he made sure that the café's door was locked and the blinds closed: he wanted to be alone with his thoughts. His visitors had pushed Lorette and the prospective poker game to the back of his mind and left him dwelling on Jamaica, the home his departed visitors thought he shared with them.

But the truth was, despite his ability to swap nostalgic recollections of that island, Boswell had no intention of ever returning to Jamaica. He was in permanent exile; London had become his home. Unlike those men, he had not been lured to London by tales of gold-paved streets or the mother country myth. In his early twenties, he had fled Jamaica after an ineffably painful discovery about his lover.

Her name was Lucy King and she was the first woman Boswell ever loved. He was working as a lowly paid clerk for a Kingston shipping company and often spent his lunch hour on the waterfront, watching the coming and going of ships in the harbour. The cruise ships with their wealthy American and European passengers always attracted a large excited crowd: skinny black boys diving in the water for coins thrown by the tourists; spectators who, like Boswell, were entranced by those seemingly unreal travellers in their linen suits, resplendent jewellery and superior airs. It was on such an occasion that he met Lucy King. The great Hollywood actress Elizabeth Maine, having recently divorced her seventh husband, was due to arrive on the *Queen Mary*. In the crowd, standing within yards of Boswell Anderson, was a young woman whose beauty could only be compared to the bird of paradise flower, fantastic, mythical almost. He instantly forgot the purpose of his presence on the dock. He went over to her, looked deep into her eyes – and what eyes! – and said: 'Let's go and sit in the sea and watch the clouds weep in the mountains.'

She did not leap at his invitation straight away, but a week later they did just that, sat in the sea near Port Royal and watched the clouds weep in the Blue Mountains. Boswell learnt that Lucy King lived with an aunt, and had recently separated from her boyfriend, Alton Clarkson. He sensed that she was still fond of Alton Clarkson, despite describing him as cruel and selfish. Clarkson had moved to Montego Bay and, Lucy said, had his sights set on migrating to New York. Her residual affection for her former lover did not trouble Boswell unduly. He was more concerned about the voracious attention Lucy received from her other admirers. Walking through Half-Way Tree or going to the Carib Theatre in Crossroads with her was like accompanying royalty. Her admirers threw kisses from across the street, called out from passing cars and delayed their passage with idle conversation which ignored Boswell's presence.

Boswell's status as a clerk, albeit a lowly paid one, gave him a huge advantage over rival suitors. Not only could he afford to take Lucy out regularly, he was willing and able to translate his passionate declarations of love into tangible gifts. He never called on her without flowers, one week bird of paradise, the next ginger lilies, then yellow roses. After the flowers he showered her with presents: a lignum vitae jewellery box, a gold ring with a heart-shaped inlay of polished black coral, a necklace of seashells encrusted with ersatz diamonds (he promised her the real thing later); and clothes imported from New York. He was simply in a different league from those rough Kingstonians: they adored Lucy King, but he worshipped her.

For a spell, Boswell's workload prevented him from seeing Lucy as often as he would have liked. Once, almost a whole month passed without him seeing her for more than a few hours. Shortly after their normal dating resumed, Lucy announced that she was pregnant. Boswell received this news with a mixture of joy and trepidation. Fatherhood was not on his agenda at this point in his life. He owned nothing, had exhausted his savings winning her love, and his meagre income could not support a family. Nevertheless, he accepted Lucy's condition, and assured her that he would stand by her like a rock.

They called the child Carl, and agreed that marriage would happen later, when Boswell's earnings increased. Two rooms on the upper floor of an old wooden house in downtown Kingston became their home. Despite the hardship Boswell found the early months of fatherhood extremely satisfying. Some nights he would lay awake, Lucy's warm body beside him, his son snoring in his cot, the smell of ripe mangoes on the nocturnal breeze, fireflies blinking in the dark, the sound of rhythm and blues music coming from a nearby bar, and he would feel happiness to perfection. On rainy Sunday afternoons they would sit on the verandah and Boswell, gazing at Lucy King's face, would say movingly: 'My love for you is like the rain, true and powerful.' Or: 'Your love makes me feel like the air after the rain, clean and fresh and invigorating.'

Lucy was less easily satisfied. She began to complain about their poverty, the faded, unfashionable dresses that she owned, the dances they could no longer afford to attend, all the Hollywood movies they were missing at the Carib Theatre. Beneath these complaints was a yearning for the life she had known before motherhood, before Boswell. In time she began to talk also of New York, where, she believed, they could make a better life for themselves. Her desire to migrate became inseparable from her litany of complaints.

Boswell did all he could to please Lucy, to make her happy. He mustered up the courage and asked his parsimonious boss for a raise and was granted a negligible one. He took to making small bets on the races at Caymanas Park and sought out card games, a pastime for which he had long nurtured a secret liking. Though he seldom lost at gambling the rewards did not match the effort.

Lucy was unmoved. Soon she began to express her increasing dissatisfaction in action. Boswell regularly arrived home to find baby Carl in the charge of their neighbour or asleep, alone, with Lucy nowhere in sight. She would sneak in late at night smelling of sweet wine, and mouthing feeble excuses about women's night out, or being delayed by the bus. Where was Lucy getting these new dresses, those new shoes; how could she leave the boy alone for such long hours, locked inside? These questions assailed Boswell as he waited for her at night. Yet on her return he said nothing, maintaining a uxorious silence.

The climax of this soured relationship crushed Boswell. One Saturday morning Lucy left home saying she was going to Port Royal. She did not return until the early hours of Monday morning. Young Carl had given Boswell a warm time, with attacks of diarrhoea and bawling for his mother, putting Boswell in a murderous mood. He had simply had enough. Calmly, holding back his rage, he told Lucy in no uncertain terms that she would have to change her ways or he would leave, taking their son whom, he was sure, he could find one of his relatives to care for until such a time as he could do it himself.

Lucy was equally calm in response to this ultimatum. She walked over to the sleeping child, picked him up with exaggerated maternal tenderness, held him to her breast, and then said to Boswell: 'You can go, but you can't take Carl because he's not your son. Is another man's child. Is Alton Clarkson's pickney.'

Boswell would remember that morning for many years, the sun rising over the distant mountains, the rustling leaves of the giant Indian mango tree that overshadowed their rooms, the faint trace of the sea in the air, the strident horns of a ship leaving the harbour, the piercing sound of a cock crowing, a dog barking. He would remember the sudden weakening of his legs, the immense hollowness in his stomach, the storm of doubts that erupted in his mind. He would remember looking at the boy, who had woken up and was squirming in his mother's arms, looking at the boy he loved, the son he thought he had fathered, and recalling the countless times he had probed the child's face and not seen a trace of his own features, only those of the mother, and hoping that time would bring about a stronger resemblance. A casual thought, a casual hope; nothing more, for he had felt secure in his fatherhood. Up until that moment.

That fateful morning he learnt that Alton Clarkson had returned to Kingston and Lucy's bed en route to New York, leaving her pregnant. She had chosen Boswell as the father because she considered him generous, gentle; because he loved her, while Clarkson was fickle and restless, completely untrustworthy.

He derived no consolation from her estimation of him as a kind fool. For days he wandered around Kingston harbour, contemplating suicide, drunk, maddened by the sorrow of betrayal. But fate was not yet finished with Boswell Anderson. Some months later, still buried in grief, nursing a deep wound which would only heal with time and other lovers – who sometimes also reopened that original wound – he left Kingston on the Spanish-owned ship the *Montserrat*. He was only vaguely aware of his destination. Escape was all that mattered. Though he would become a master of nostalgic badinage to homesick immigrants in cold, lonely London, a teller of fantastic tales which originated in his imagination; encouraging his customers to confide in him, to reveal the pain in their hearts, he himself never seriously held any dreams of going back home. Nor would he ever divulge his reason for leaving Jamaica. It was his secret. It was hidden behind the happy-go-lucky mask. He would take it to his grave.

Now, in the Caribbean Sunset Café, he looked at the cheque Bobby Summers had given him, hoped it wouldn't bounce, and smiled in appreciation of this unexpected windfall which would go towards the poker game at Stone Mason's table. He folded it, put it in his wallet; then he left the café.

Boswell was reluctant to go home just yet; he could not bear to smell that odour again. He decided to stop in the Lord Nelson pub. He would play a few hands of dominoes, hang out at the bar. Perhaps Tom Redcam, the landlord, could distract him with his much-told tales about his Second World War adventures. Yes, that seemed the best way to spend the evening; though he, Boswell, knew that the greatest war man has to fight is with his heart.

Chapter Six

Gilbert Singh was sitting on Hackney Downs reflecting on the ruins of his life. Somewhere nearby, somebody banged on a piano and a car horn blasted and the discordant notes assaulted his already frayed nerves. Above the leafless horse chestnut trees, in the near distance, the concrete tower blocks of the Nightingale Estate, their peaks crowned by an overcast, cottony sky, looked down on Gilbert – or so it seemed to him – with solemn disapproval, judging and sentencing him from their silent height. At the other extreme of the downs, a blue and red train streaked across elevated tracks and disappeared into the wilderness of buildings that were the city. A group of mothers pushing their pram-bound, thumb-sucking, sullen-faced children approached along the path. Passing Gilbert, they surveyed him with what seemed like fear and pity. He lowered his head until they were some yards away, then raised it and rubbed the white bristle of his unshaved face, as if in their passing the mothers had suddenly made him conscious of his personal dereliction. His body, caked in sweat, itched, smelt, and his joints ached. His mouth felt clammy.

'Oh, Sushi, why you do me so?' Gilbert moaned. A week ago Sushi, Gilbert's wife, called by her sickly younger sister, had travelled to Birmingham. She would be away for at least a month; they had not spent a night apart in twenty-five years. Though Gilbert had given his wholehearted support to her mercy mission, he had not anticipated the devastating effects of her absence on his own wellbeing. In the early hours of his second morning alone, he had reached out for her warm, corpulent body and fallen into the abyss of her absence.

That evening, unable to face another night alone, he had visited Lucky Morgan, a fellow habitué of several Hackney bookmakers. They had finished a bottle of rum and would have opened another but around midnight Lucky Morgan's wife had stormed into the living room and demanded her husband's immediate presence in bed. In short, she had evicted Gilbert. Drunk and lonesome, walking home along Morning Lane, he had encountered a Dundus.

It had leapt out from between parked cars and stood before him, a luminous devil-like creature with Medusa-like hair, shoulder-length, each strand millions of writhing bodies, the souls of mortals it had devoured. It had inspired such fear in Gilbert that he had fled home and drunk himself to sleep, waking up the following afternoon only to buy more liquor to help him survive the night. Now able to face the cold light of day, he saw the Dundus as a warning. Sushi had sent it to ensure that he behaved himself while she was away. 'Oh, Sushi, why you do me so?' Gilbert moaned.

He asked the time of a man passing by with a Rottweiler. It disturbed him to learn that it was almost midday, which meant he had been sitting on the bench for over two hours. I've got to hold myself together, he thought. He decided to go home and clean himself up. Afterwards he would drop in on the bookmaker's, and then the Caribbean Sunset Café. Maybe I can persuade Bosy to come home and share a bottle of Scotch, he thought. He did not want to spend another night alone.

Gilbert regarded Boswell as his closest friend, his adviser and confidant. It was Boswell to whom he complained when Sushi, as she did frequently, admonished him for wasting his life in the bookmaker's. Boswell invariably gave him sympathy, and advised him on how to get his ways with Sushi. But this was by no means a friendship between unequals. Gilbert's knowledge of the horses was far superior to Boswell's, especially since marriage seemed to have cooled Boswell's passion for gambling. So as Gilbert – suffering from excess freedom and its consequent loneliness – walked home, the prospect of sitting down with his old friend over a bottle of Scotch, talking politics and sharing memories of friends, cheered him immeasurably.

By the time Gilbert reached the Caribbean Sunset Café, he was feeling much better. But he found only Mona sitting behind the counter. She was, as usual, flicking through her romance magazine.

'How's my sweetness?' Gilbert said.

'Fine.'

'Where's Bosy, in the back?'

'No. He left about ten minutes ago. Said he'd return in an hour.'

'Leave you in charge. Must really trust you.'

Mona did not respond. Gilbert ordered a cup of tea. Seated now in the Caribbean Sunset Café, Gilbert felt good. Boswell would soon return, and he was sure that his old friend would not pass up the opportunity to share a bottle of whisky.

Time passed at an interminable pace, and soon after Gilbert had started on a third cup of tea the telephone rang. Mona answered it and Gilbert heard her saying, 'Yes, yes,' like a child taking instructions. He heard his name mentioned, then she called him to the telephone, saying: 'It's Bosy. He wants to talk to you.'

Gilbert took the phone and said with the petulance of a lover who has been kept waiting, 'Bosy, where are you, man?'

'I'm tied up. Can't make it back for another few hours. Make sure Mona lock up properly for me. Do that for me, Gilbert.'

'No problem, man. When you finish come round to the house later, nuh?'

'I'll try. But look for me late.'

Gilbert reassured Boswell that he would supervise Mona while she locked up. Half an hour later Gilbert himself locked up the Caribbean Sunset Café and gave the keys to Mona, who had protested that the locks were too stiff.

It was a fine evening. Spring was in the air and the starlings which nested in a derelict building on Chatsworth Road were in full song, shrill even above the traffic noise. It had been an overcast day, but the clouds had cleared to reveal a pale blue sky. A few yards from the Caribbean Sunset Café an ornamental cherry tree had blossomed early and its pink colours enlivened the drab street where market traders were packing away their wares. Gilbert was touched by all this, the seasons in transit, day winding down, and as he turned to say goodbye to Mona it occurred to him that they could stroll a part of the way home together. He proposed this to Mona and she agreed, with an indifferent 'OK'. Gilbert was delighted.

With Mona walking, close and silent, beside him, Gilbert began to feel a curious mixture of elation and wistfulness. Memories of the banana plantation in Jamaica where he had grown up flooded his mind. The luxuriant greenness of the morning, the dew dripping off the broad leaves like beads of quicksilver, sparkling when struck by sunlight; those broad leaves, now translucent, now a deep brooding green and always tranquil, irenic; a favourite tree where he as a boy had sometimes paused to pluck a plump yellow finger, strip it and eat it there and it would taste like a piece of the sun; the magic of the banana shoots, a majestic purple, springing from seemingly dead stumps – these memories struck him true and sharp and powerfully.

'You ever see a banana plantation, Mona?' Gilbert asked.

'I've seen a big field of banana trees,' Mona replied flatly.

'A truly beautiful thing,' Gilbert said. He shared with her the images that swam in his memory. When Mona sighed with the recognition and longing of someone who knew the landscape of his past, Gilbert was further surprised. He had never seen Mona express any emotions, and her unexpected response spurred him on to more exalted recollections of an idyll all the more idyllic because he had not experienced it in almost thirty years.

They were approaching the street where Gilbert lived, and where they should have gone their separate ways, as Mona lived further on. But Gilbert was by now so intoxicated on his memories that he was reluctant to part with Mona. She had been a good companion on their brief stroll; he had glimpsed a side to her character that her colourless, stolid behaviour at work concealed. Nor did she appear to be in a hurry to leave him. Though she remained expressionless, he felt a warmth emanating from her, as if she, too, were enjoying herself. So he invited her to his basement flat. Again he was surprised at how readily she agreed. It now struck Gilbert that Mona would agree to anything he asked of her. Anything.

Less than an hour later Gilbert showed Mona the door of his home. She was leaving with the same impassive expression that she had entered with, as though they had merely had tea together. But Gilbert was shaking slightly and his fore-head glistened with the sweat caused by his exertions, and a modicum of fear.

'You won't tell anybody, will you, Mona?' Gilbert said anxiously, thinking of Sushi and Boswell.

Mona looked at him with her large brown innocent eyes which seemed to say, 'Tell anybody what?'

When Mona reached street level, Gilbert closed the front door, bolted and double-locked it, checked that all the windows were locked; then headed straight for the bottle of Scotch he had wanted to share with Boswell. The drink would help to still his fear that Boswell or, far more importantly, Sushi, might discover his misdemeanour. But it would be less effective in quietening the elation provoked by Mona or his desire for another encounter with her. Her dark, downy body became inseparable from the island he had known: her eyes were its rivers, her scent its dusks, her body its nights. She had touched him deeply, provoked memories and revived dreams that would sleep no more.

He half finished the bottle and fell into a slumber as near to oblivion as the edge of the world. He almost did not hear Boswell, who had come to collect the café's keys, ringing his doorbell.

Gilbert Singh was the scion of a wealthy family of banana planters. His great-grandfather Vijay Singh I was a legendary figure in the banana-growing villages in the Portland foothills of the Blue Mountains. Vijay Singh I went to Jamaica as an indentured labourer and died a rich centenarian, leaving behind a son whom he'd bludgeoned into sycophantic timidity and a beloved grandson, Vijay Roy Singh, Gilbert's father, to whom he bequeathed his two-hundred-acre banana plantation.

When Vijay Roy Singh named his first son Gilbert he took an unforgivable leap from tradition. The first-born male child in the family had always been named Vijay. One of the old man's last pronouncements was that the boy would suffer because he had not been given a name which reflected his lineage. Ironically, though, it was Vijay Roy Singh's defiance of the old man which made him overlook his grandson, along with the timid son, and pass on his wealth to his great-grandson.

Gilbert's father had great ambitions for him. He could see which way the wind was blowing and predicted independence for Jamaica before he died. Not having had much of an education, Vijay Roy Singh decided to invest in Gilbert. His son would be both a wealthy farmer and a politician. With that glorious future in mind, Vijay Roy Singh imposed a remorselessly harsh regime of studies on the boy, keeping him up until midnight to learn by rote the lessons that would eventually transform the Singhs from well-to-do farmers into a sophisticated modern family.

At the age of eleven Gilbert was dispatched to Mica College in Kingston and returned home only during the holidays. But three years later a hurricane wiped out a season's crop and the bank foreclosed on loans. Confronted with a crisis, a considerably poorer Vijay Roy Singh rediscovered the virtues of his late grandfather's parsimonious habits. He resented the expenses he was having to lavish on Gilbert's education and capriciously decided that it was time for the boy to enter the college of life.

From precious schoolboy with feminine hands, Gilbert was transformed into a machete-wielding, sweat-soaked, foul-mouthed plantation worker whose working day ended over a bottle of white rum. He had a past to live down. So he worked and swore harder than his companions. One day a drunk called him a dirty coolie and he chased the man with a machete halfway to Port Antonio. This incident earned him respect and notoriety and soon enough the attention of the village girls.

Enter Victoria. She stole Gilbert's heart with kisses that were sweeter than a Julie mango and twice as watery. She cast a deep spell of love over him. She ensnared him with teasing romps through the banana fields, allowed him only the lightest of kisses beneath those translucent leaves, and early one morning below the waterfall of the Rio Grande transported him to an unexplored height of pleasure. A five-hundred-year-old cotton tree, which the whole village feared because of the ancient stories about ghosts and spirits, became their meeting place. An amorous temple where Gilbert would hold and kiss Victoria and feel like a man, strong and virile and in control of his life.

When Vijay Roy Singh heard that his eldest son and heir to the family business was cavorting with a Negress, he immediately arranged the boy's marriage. Gilbert was eighteen and way past the date when he should have married. The family found a fifteen-year-old girl in Oracabessa and gave a heifer for her. After the deal had been arranged Gilbert was introduced to his wife.

At first Vijay Roy Singh met his son's protestation with diplomacy. He appealed to him by talking of the pride of the family and how he once saw himself building a dynasty and it was not too late to achieve that. His mother, Parma, reminded Gilbert how she had carried him for nine months and then endured a pain that he as a man would never know in order to bring him into this world; how she wiped his backside and sucked the cold from his nose. Gilbert angered his father with a brief show of defiance, outright refusal, which was interpreted as insolence, treachery and wickedness. Then Vijay Roy Singh played his last card: he threatened to disown and disinherit him. He gave Gilbert a day to decide.

Gilbert did not need a whole day. He had been due to meet Victoria at the cotton tree that night. But as he made his way there through the dense tropical darkness, which seemed to mirror his own future, and a nocturnal cacophony which echoed the babel of voices in his head, he was enfeebled by an attack of cowardliness. He ran back home, tearing through the bush like a man who had seen his own ghost. He was no pioneer. He would follow the tried and trusted path trod by his father, grandfather and great-grandfather.

So he married Sushi, the stranger from Oracabessa. Months later he began to hear the rumour: Victoria's family had sent her away because she was pregnant. He went to visit the family of his former lover and possibly mother of his first child, to find out the truth. But her brothers, sisters, parents and cousins chased him away with the sticks and stones of their shame.

By and by Gilbert seemed to forget Victoria. For the next few years he dedicated himself to work on the plantation and various correspondence courses from London colleges. Unknown to everyone Gilbert was plotting escape from the bondages of family and tradition, and a past of which he was unspeakably ashamed.

His long nights poring over books under the light of the kerosene lamp were rewarded with passes in Part One of the City and Guilds examination in mechanical engineering. This pleased Vijay Roy Singh immensely, as he had diversified the family business into trucking; his dreams of patrician greatness were revived. He did not hesitate to sponsor Gilbert's course of studies in mechanical engineering in London.

Within months of arriving in London Gilbert abandoned his studies and began a swift descent into the twilight world of gamblers and hustlers. His father soon severed his monthly allowance, forcing Gilbert to live off his wits. Cheated in a card game which left him stony-broke, Gilbert suffered a nervous breakdown and was hospitalised for a month. He discharged himself, but his nerves would remain poor for ever. There would be days when Gilbert's eyes, sunken and encircled by dark stains, had the intensity of someone walking the thin line between sanity and insanity.

One day he returned home to his tiny bedsit in Archway and found Sushi squatting outside the door as if she were sitting in the dust beside the hut back in the village from which Vijay Roy Singh had plucked her. The letter that should have warned him of her arrival came three days later. He shared the bedsit with her for a week, sleeping on the floor while she occupied the bed. Then he ordered her to find somewhere else to live and leave him alone.

But Sushi would not be intimidated. 'Me is you wife, you damn foolish coolie,' Sushi said. 'You can't throw me away like you throw away dat neygah gal.' Sushi's remark so enraged Gilbert that he tried to attack her. But months of malnourishment had left him too weak for this robust country girl. She gave him a thorough thrashing and then took control of his life.

Sushi proved herself to be so strong and resourceful and faithful that he ceased to resent her. A part of Gilbert became resigned to the fact that his life was never meant to be his in the first place; all the agony he had endured had been caused by his pursuit of a freedom which was not destined for him. But he was uncompromising in his determination never to return to Jamaica. He became an exile of the worst sort: one who punished others by punishing himself.

By the time they moved into Homerton, Gilbert had made several irreversible transitions, from student to worker, from worker to gambler. He lacked the nerves required for a successful poker player but made a modest income from the horses.

He discovered the Caribbean Sunset Café in the days when he still played poker. He found kindred spirits there. He frequented its blues dances, always alone, and whiled away his afternoons in nostalgic conversations about home, about Jamaica, with men and women who shared his passion for the island. Its regular customers embraced him as one of their own. They called him simply Singh. Singh was a wild drinker, a reckless poker player, a character who could be relied upon to enliven a dull afternoon with ribald tales and graphic, evocative descriptions of the Jamaica he knew. Everybody loved Singh.

Now and again Gilbert thought about Victoria and the son he heard she had given birth to. On those occasions his behaviour, fuelled by regret and remorse, became even more extreme, and the customers of the Caribbean Sunset Café would whisper behind his back, 'De coolie mahn gone mad.'

One afternoon he confessed all to a gathering of acquaintances. He told them about his father and Victoria, told his story with such feeling, such sorrow, that he and several listeners were moved to tears. Boswell had to close the Caribbean Sunset Café earlier than usual that day because long after Gilbert Singh had departed the sorrow of his story saturated the air, like the smell of burning sugar cane, sweet and acrid and angry. And for the next six months there were daily spontaneous confessions from other customers who had some secret from back home, from the diverse islands of their origins, to unburden. Like that of the Barbadian who had impregnated his stepdaughter; the Dominican mother who had killed her baby in a fit of anger because its bawling disturbed her and her lover; the Jamaican who had abandoned his prodigiously fertile wife because every time he touched her she became pregnant and when the ninth child came along decided that the call of the mother country was an irresistibly simple solution to this unremitting deluge of children; the St Lucian whose wife had left him for a woman; the Grenadian whose father wrote him daily letters accusing him of abandonment, desertion and parricide – and all of them missed their island homes, pined for them in their exiled hearts. But it was Gilbert Singh's eloquently and movingly told tale of betrayed love which started these confessions of the heart which once helped to make the Caribbean Sunset Café a very special place.

Chapter Seven

Boswell's campaign to raise funds for the forthcoming poker game was gathering momentum. The unexpected cheque from Bobby Summers had been supplemented by the repayment of another loan, this time from Lance Johnson, whom he had met in the Lord Nelson pub three nights ago. Lance Johnson was notorious for denying his debts but he had handed over some cash without argument, and Boswell took this as a good omen. He was not sure what to make of Lance's tale about reforming his ways after encountering, late at night, a man, or something, wearing a floor-length cloak of peacock feathers with 'a million accusing eyes' and a hideous wooden mask. He had advised Lance to abstain from whatever drug he was consuming.

As it was the end of the month, Boswell was now settling down behind the café's counter to do his accounts. He reached into his pocket and felt not a pen, but paper. He pulled it out and was shocked to see Cleo's letter, unopened, unread weeks since he had received it. He figured that the dry-cleaner must have extracted it and then replaced it where he found it in the clean suit.

He poured himself a glass of Scotch from the bottle he kept for visitors, opened the letter and began to read.

My Dearest Boswell,

I hope you are in robust good health. It has been ages since we corresponded and I must take some of the blame for that, as you wrote last. I hope you will forgive my silence over the past few years after reading this long overdue letter.

Remember how for years upon years I used to assail you with the details of my wonderful married life in

St Ann? Remember how I used to describe Gladstone McDonald as the sort of man every woman dreamt of, handsome, gentle, intelligent, humorous, sensitive, loving, charming? Remember the three children whose births I told you about in joyous letters? Remember the citrus orchard that I tried to lure you back to?

It's all gone now, Boswell. Everything's gone like a puff of smoke, as if it had been a cruel magical interlude of happiness in a life fated for misery. In this, the evening of my life, I have to start all over again.

I am writing this letter in a room which comes with my housemaid job in a New York apartment which is larger than any house I have ever lived in. It belongs to the Goldsteins who are big in television or something like that. I wash clothes and dishes and generally keep the place clean. When Mrs Goldstein is entertaining I have to wear a white and blue uniform with a red bandana. Mrs Goldstein insists that I look very becoming in it, but it's as uncomfortable as hell. But I should not complain too much. The work is light and the pay reasonable. I am able to send money home for the children every month. They live with my youngest sister Pamsy in Port Antonio. Gladstone is somewhere in America. I'll get to him later.

Some of my past letters painted a rosier picture than was really the case. I did not, for instance, tell you about the troubles I was having with my Dorothy. She is my first daughter. I can see the shock on your face, as I never mentioned her during our time together. I couldn't; you are not the only one with a secret, Boswell. Dorothy was born while I was still in school, which as you can well imagine scandalised my very respectable family. The boy, the father, disappeared as soon as he heard I was pregnant. Uptil today I don't know what became of him.

My parents took me out of school before the pregnancy began to show, and I was sent to a distant cousin of my mother's in Savanna la Mar. Immediately after giving birth I came home, leaving the baby behind. I was required to forget that I was a mother for the family's reputation. A terrible silence of shame surrounded the whole episode, and I colluded with it. I really believed that no man would seriously consider marrying a woman who had become a mother in such disgraceful circumstances. And, you know, for a long while I succeeded in forgetting Dorothy.

That's why I did not tell you about her. She really did not exist for me. With Marvin's birth everything changed. The joy I felt holding him in my arms, Boswell, the joy. Yet Marvin also brought sadness. His birth ripped off the scabs of my amnesia and the pus exposed how wicked and callous I had been, how much I had suffered and caused the suffering of my own flesh and blood.

But what could I do? I hadn't told Gladstone about Dorothy and to tell him then would have seemed as if I had deceived him into marriage. So I began to search for a way of being reunited with my daughter and eventually decided that I would get her to live with me without her or Gladstone knowing that she was really my child. When Ella was born I began to find fault in our maid and discussed with Gladstone the possibility of bringing in the daughter of my distant cousin in Savanna la Mar. We could school her in exchange for some housework. Gladstone left the decision up to me. The house, he always said, was my realm.

So I brought her home, Boswell, brought Dorothy home, brought my daughter home after nearly thirteen years. Spontaneously, a warm intimacy developed between us. She was like a younger sister. When I became pregnant again, with Otis, she practically mothered me. Such was her devotion, her care, her affection. I used to wonder whether she knew. Sometimes I would get fearful with this thought because I worried that perhaps she was scheming to exact revenge for my abandoning her and then continuing to deny her. The fear of a guilty mother. But it did not surface often enough to disturb the happiness we enjoyed together.

Things began to fall apart shortly after I gave birth to

Otis, my youngest. Dorothy was now sixteen and pretty in the way I was pretty before I began to put on weight, much of which, incidentally, I have lost in the maelstrom of the last few years. She worked part time at the St Ann post office.

One day she told me that Gladstone had tried to molest her. You can imagine my alarm, anger and then dilemma. I had created this illusion of family harmony and all of a sudden it was threatening to disintegrate. I had no reason to disbelieve Dorothy. She had proven herself a faithful, loyal and honest child. I trusted her completely.

No. I exaggerate. It did occur to me that she was trying to destroy my family, drive a wedge between me and Gladstone by sowing the seeds of mistrust. That was one reason why I hesitated for such a long time before acting. The other reason was I really did not know what to do. When Dorothy repeated her charge I had to act.

Gladstone, of course, denied everything with violent indignation. In fact, he said it was Dorothy who was always flaunting her body like some Kingston whore. For months the house was like a battlefield. Dorothy would not speak to Gladstone or remain for one moment in the same room and seemed to believe that I took his side. At the same time Gladstone was demanding that I send her away because she had become too feisty. She showed him no respect. Meanwhile, Otis, who suffers from asthma, was demanding my attention night and day.

Finally, for the sake of peace, I sent Dorothy to live with a grandaunt in Kingston. It was a painful decision to make. I agonised over it for months. But it was either her or Gladstone and I could not drive the children's father away. Oh, Boswell, if only you knew how many sleepless nights I endured wrestling with my conscience, how sharp and painful the stones along the road that brought me to that decision. To send Dorothy away again after all those years. Even now, Boswell, I die a little each night in a sleep that seems like an eternal punishment.

By and by things settled down in the house. I began to feel less guilty about Dorothy when she wrote saying that she liked Kingston. I worried, of course, that she might go astray there. But she was a sensible girl and my grandaunt with whom she lived was strict enough to ensure that she stayed that way. Following my advice she enrolled in a secretarial college and I paid the fees.

But it was not long before another storm rushed in off the sea. Gladstone was a competent manager of the orchard so I can't blame him for the devastation wrought by the citrus bug. We lost over half the trees. We were lucky. Some people lost everything and eventually gave away their land. We had a large piece of land separated from the main farm by a copse and then a stony tract, and on a hill. I thought it strange that Gladstone didn't seem too worried by the bug. I soon found out why. One day, Gladstone suddenly announced that he had to go to Miami, supposedly to buy a strain of oranges trees that were resistant to the bug. Less than twenty-four hours after his departure, the house and farm were swarming with police and soldiers in jeeps and helicopters buzzed overhead. To my horror I learnt that Gladstone had been farming over ten acres of ganja for years, and lodging the profit in a Miami bank account. Not only that, he had emptied our own joint account.

Boswell, I was broken, broken in heart, broken in spirit and broken in mind. I could not think straight. I did not want to live. The first offer I received for the orchard I took it and bought a small house in Port Antonio for the children. I have been in New York for about eighteen months now. When I am not working, I go about making enquiries for Gladstone McDonald. I will find him. So help me God, I will find him. He must help look after our children.

Next month Dorothy is getting married. Will I go to the wedding? I don't know, Boswell. I still have not told her that she is my daughter, though I suspect that she knows. She was among the first to send her sympathy when

61

she heard of my misfortune, even offered to give up college to be on hand to help. I refused.

Please write and let me know how life has treated you since your last letter. And, Boswell, don't pity me. I am alive. I am healthy and I intend to see the last of my children into adulthood before I enter the next world.

Yours, with abiding love, Cleo.

Finished, Boswell carefully – as carefully as his shaking hands allowed – folded Cleo's letter and put it in his back pocket. He would not get home until way past midnight. He would spend hours remembering Cleo, the woman whose love, many years before, had saved him from certain early death and helped to create the Caribbean Sunset Café. He would try to understand the implications of the contents of her letter. For their fates, he knew from past experience, were inextricably bound together.

He had been in London for five restless years and lived in and off the underbelly of the city. He slept during the day, and at night haunted gambling dens all over London. If the capricious god of the night was kind to him, blessed him with full houses and flushes and reckless opponents, he would wake up in the perfumed arms of a woman whose avowed undying affections expired with his last pound. Many nights' loss and sudden impecuniosity compelled him to walk lonely streets. The next day he would dust himself down, don his mask of incorrigible optimism and plunge back into the fray. Soberness, empty hours and solitude only caused him to remember Jamaica and the cause of his flight from the island.

Cleo rescued him from himself, lured him from the edge of the abyss. They met one night at a wild party thrown by Wally Fletcher to celebrate the anniversary of Jamaican independence. Wally Fletcher, a high red Jamaican from the island's plantocracy, had been rusticated from the LSE and was hopelessly addicted to gambling and the company of artists and hustlers. Cleo had cooked the food, and hers was the most powerful voice when the party suddenly lifted off with a lusty rendition of 'Dig a Hole':

> God made the bee and the bee made honey,
> God made man and man made money.
> We gonna dig a hole, dig a hole
> And put the devil in.

Boswell had stood beside her in the singing and when it finished he said, to nobody in particular, with a pained longing: 'I used to sit in the sea and watch the clouds weep in the mountains.' They passed the rest of the evening in each other's company, exchanging memories of back home.

With a complexion as dark as polished black coral, a gargantuan figure and a sad raspy voice, she was not the sort of woman Boswell would normally look at twice. He liked his women slim, but not too slim. And he preferred women a shade or two lighter than Cleo. So at the end of the night he could not understand why he was feeling so excited about her invitation to visit her when he wished, or why this excitement survived his discovery on reaching home that he had lost his keys and had to wake up his querulous landlord, or why he was subsequently so indignant when his friend Bobby Summers asked with a lascivious grin: 'Who was dat fat pussy you were talking to all night at Wally's place, man?'

Bobby Summers' disparaging remark did not deter Boswell from calling on Cleo a week after meeting her. He might have gone there thinking he would get a quick easy lay. But he was soon disabused of that idea. The honesty of his intention would be tested. He discovered that Cleo, too, had lost her keys on the night of Wally Fletcher's party. To their dismay and amazement, this coincidental misfortune was repeated several times during the incipient stage of their friendship. On the same night that Boswell was evicted from his room for a small fortune in rent arrears Cleo was given notice to quit by her landlord, ostensibly because he wanted her room for a relative. Then Boswell suffered a severe attack of gastro-enteritis and Cleo a vicious bout of influenza which caused her to lose a stone in weight, though the loss could only be detected by the most discerning eyes. The climax came when both Boswell and Cleo were knocked down by hit-and-run drivers in separate incidents miles apart. Cleo wasn't hurt but she was hospitalised for a week suffering from shock, and Boswell's shoulder was dislocated.

Gladstone McDonald warned Cleo that Boswell was not only a harbinger of bad luck, he was also a dangerous irresponsible refugee from the crime-infested tenement yards of downtown Kingston. But it was in Gladstone's interest to traduce Boswell's name: he had been courting Cleo until Boswell intruded, and reacted to their growing intimacy with the proprietorial ferocity of a gold prospector who had discovered the mother lode.

Who was Gladstone McDonald? Gladstone was a bombastic fellow from Montego Bay who walked around with a photograph of himself attending a Macdonald Clan reunion as incontrovertible proof of his Scottish ancestry. Although he had abandoned the law studies that had brought him to London, having repeatedly failed the exams, Gladstone still boastfully referred to himself as a student of jurisprudence.

For a while the two men jostled for Cleo's affection. If by chance Boswell and Gladstone met in Cleo's room, neither would want to leave first, even if this meant staying up half the night and inconveniencing their hostess. To impress Cleo, Gladstone would attempt to discourse at length on topical issues of the day, citing from *The Times* and using the recondite language of his aborted discipline.

The sports pages and the racing forms of the popular newspapers were the extent of Boswell's reading habits. But he was a man of the streets, and instinctively recognised the pretentiousness of his rival. Boswell himself advised Gladstone in one of their many frosty exchanges, 'Nuh put you'self inna barrel when matchbox can hol' you.'

Gladstone soon disappeared from the field, bowled out by the uncanny rapport between Cleo and Boswell, as well as

Boswell's refusal to be intimidated by the superior airs of the failed advocate.

With Gladstone out of the way, there began between Boswell and Cleo a romance that would change his life. He had never known anyone like Cleo. She belonged to an entirely different world from the Caribbean demimonde of which he was a fully paid-up member. She had come to London from a well-to-do family in St Ann to study nursing and dropped out on discovering what seemed like a congenital aversion to the sight of blood.

The fellows in Boswell's circle called her Mama Cleo on account of her size. The good-time women, starved of Boswell's patronage, spread rumours that Cleo had bewitched him with obeah, with soup laced with her vaginal juices. None of those fellows could imagine the endless hours of pleasure Cleo's prodigious body gave him, the constant discovery of jelly-like flesh that quivered in delight at his touch; the incomparable love of a fat woman. As for those jealous rumour-mongers, they could never understand that a man in his walk of life – where self-confidence and every penny in his pocket could disappear at the flick of a card – valued loyalty far more than conventional beauty.

Cleo was certainly loyal. She welcomed Boswell regardless of the state of his finances. Her passions were narrow but deep and pursued with imperturbable serenity. She was a compulsive letter writer and could spend weeks composing a missive to a friend in Jamaica or America. Watching her engaged in this epistolary pastime sometimes provoked in Boswell a curious eroticism. Like a boy unable to resist the urge to disturb the stillness of a pond, he often playfully tempted her away from her task and on to the bed, where they could compose together.

But he did not find all Cleo's habits so attractive. Boswell was a spare eater, one meal a day was enough for him. Cleo was a gourmand of Jamaican dishes, savoury and sweet, and spent an inordinate amount of time cooking and eating. One weekend Cleo consumed three pounds of fried steak, a whole chicken, six lamb chops, an entire baking tray of sweet potato pudding, a whole banana cake, a gallon of ice cream, a jug of carrot juice, a dozen oranges and three pomegranates. In between this feverish feast she somehow managed to conclude a letter she had been writing for weeks and engage Boswell in a lovemaking session which was so uplifting that he spoke in tongues for hours afterwards.

On the Monday after that astonishing feat Cleo received a telegram from Jamaica informing her of the death of her parents in a road accident. She flew to Jamaica the following day.

Her absence gave Boswell time to reflect on the strange territory into which he had strayed. In the brief time he had known Cleo she had persuaded him to open a savings account, to avoid squandering his winnings on the flashy ephemera of victory. In the privacy of her company, the happy-go-lucky mask he wore in public could slip and the real Boswell Anderson, a deeply melancholy and ruminative person, could breathe without embarrassment. If he had not revealed to her the cause of his flight to London, it was because she seemed blissfully incurious about his past. Indeed, she had intimated that coming to London was for her a new beginning, though what wrong such an apparently innocent, almost seraphic person could have committed was beyond his imagination. He was temperamentally disinclined to plan too far but a future with Cleo was not an unappealing prospect.

Shortly after Cleo returned to London – showing no signs of bereavement – she won a transistor radio in an office raffle. This was the start of Boswell's upturn. An extraordinary chain of successes at the bookmaker's and on the poker table suddenly swelled his wallet. Within weeks he had substantial savings, five pairs of bespoke shoes of such fine quality that it seemed a shame to soil them on the city pavements, and an equal number of suits tailored by Burt Xavier.

But with money came acrimony. Cleo began to talk about marriage and going home to St Ann where she had been left a large piece of land with over two hundred amazingly fecund orange and grapefruit trees that were being reclaimed by the bush. The longer Boswell's winning streak lasted, the more pressing Cleo's desire for marriage, for children, for mornings impregnated with the sharp sweet scent of the citrus orchard.

When he realised the depth of her sincerity, the strength of her dream, he attempted to appease her with gold and ivory jewellery. On one particularly extravagant occasion he hired a private room in a Soho Chinese restaurant and gave Cleo a free run of the menu. The meal lasted for only ten hours because the restaurant staff were exhausted. These propitiatory gifts, substitutes for the one desire he was powerless to satisfy, had little effect on Cleo. Her dream was priceless. Cleo, once so companionable, now destroyed one of the virtues that made her attractive to Boswell: her lack of interest in his past. She demanded to know why he would not go home with her. Had he abandoned wife and children there? Was he wanted by the law? Depending on his mood he answered these persistent questions with a playful tenderness intended to distract her, or a violent silence to signal his impatience.

Cleo's unrelenting questions drove Boswell back into his old habits. He began to haunt the night, the bottle and the strange beds of loveless, unloving women. Then early one morning after an especially dissolute night, crawling towards home – then in Finsbury Park – along Chatsworth Road, he noticed a building with a For Sale sign. Inspiration struck him like a bolt of lightning. He imagined himself and Cleo running a little grocery store which sold West Indian food, or a little café like the Italians and Spaniards did.

Later that same day, having removed most of his savings, Boswell signed a twenty-year lease on the building (he would later buy it outright). That very evening he persuaded a reluctant Cleo to accompany him to see it. Its grimy walls, its broken windows, its tragic air, must have convinced her that there was no hope. A near-derelict building in Hackney stood no comparison with even a single dew-laden orange tree. She wailed and railed for two days and then expelled Boswell for ever from her body and room and life. He protested, of course, sent her flowers and boxes of exotic chocolate. But all to no avail. Then Cleo suddenly vanished, leaving only rumours that she had become engaged to Gladstone McDonald.

It was Cleo's longing for Jamaica which inspired the name: the Caribbean Sunset Café. This was emblazoned across the window in an arch, with colourful letters resembling pieces of bamboo.

A year later Boswell received his first letter from Cleo. It confirmed that she had married Gladstone McDonald and revealed that they had moved to Jamaica, to the citrus orchard in St Ann. She was pregnant and looking forward to a happy life and wished that he, Boswell, would one day exorcise whatever demon made him such a lonely and, she feared, self-destructive person. He almost cried when he received that letter. Not because Cleo had married – he had by then become reconciled to her absence, to having lost her – but because she had the generosity of heart to concern herself with his emotional wellbeing. It took him three months and countless visits to the library to compose a reply. Since then they had corresponded regularly, with Boswell saving Cleo's letters in a small suitcase, which he kept in the Caribbean Sunset Café.

Chapter Eight

Since that strange night of the burglary Blake had not gone beyond half a mile of his flat. A debilitating lethargy had descended on him. Even the rented videos of action films with which he filled his days were watched without enthusiasm. His brother, Barry, and his mother, Carmen, had continued to prey on his mind. Between thinking about them, he replayed endlessly those few intense minutes of fear and sex in Highgate. He felt as though he had taken some potent drug and its shortlived high had been followed by this long-drawn-out low, where nothing made any sense.

Today, though, he could not afford to hang around his flat. He had to sign on at the unemployment office. He set out a little after one o'clock. The open air rekindled his taste for life. He decided that he would look up Boswell and other friends after signing on. Perhaps he would tell them about his adventure – the woman, the thing in the golden cape. No, he decided, he wouldn't tell anybody about the bizarre thing he had seen – who would believe him? – and he definitely wouldn't tell Boswell about the burglary; that would invite a long lecture. Only his other friends would appreciate his Highgate adventure. As he walked he embellished the story, transformed the seductress into a sex-starved middle-class housewife who had begged him and he had reluctantly agreed. He imagined the laughter and admiration of his friends, and this cheered him up. With his optimism revived he was determined to make some money. He had about a hundred pounds' worth of Moroccan black and if he sold it all by the end of the day, his diminishing cash would be replenished.

He passed gangs of forlorn teenagers milling about in the square. The boys all wore thick-soled ankle-high trainers and baggy jeans, and their almost shaved heads were elaborately patterned as if with tribal marks. The girls wore multi-coloured Lycra tights that accentuated the shape of their hard little bums. A boy from one of the gangs came to greet Blake. Their fists touched and they exchanged a few words. Then the boy strutted back to the company of his friends, triumphantly, as if he had just proven his familiarity with a person of importance.

Blake carried on, his self-esteem bolstered by the boy's fawning respect. The boy also stirred a pleasant nostalgia for the empty carefree days when he hung about without intent or purpose, talking about girls and football and music. When the nostalgia passed a light sadness settled over him, as he remembered that he would soon be visiting Barry. He did not want to think about Barry just then, did not want the sadness which accompanied all his thoughts on his brother. So he thought instead of the guys he would meet in The Hole, the story he would tell, the hash he wanted to sell by the end of the day.

After signing on – a five-minute exercise – he made his way to the Caribbean Sunset Café. He had planned to spend an hour or so there with Boswell. It was empty, and the Boswell who sat behind the counter smoking seemed like a stranger, distant, morose and indifferent to his presence. Nothing Blake said could spark a conversation. He had not seen Boswell in such a slough of despond since the year he, Boswell, and Carmen broke up. But even then Boswell had been welcoming, talkative, as if in talking he were trying to chase away his blues. Blake stayed for twenty minutes, then headed for The Hole. Boswell barely acknowledged his departure.

The Hole was a long narrow low-ceilinged basement behind Lower Clapton Road. When he arrived there the poker players had already assembled and Busby the mechanic and Dreadie occupied the sole pool table. Blake sold two pieces of hash to some poker players and another piece to Busby the mechanic. Dreadie wasn't interested; in strict accordance with his religion he only smoked the holy weed.

Soon Mikey B. strutted in. He was a handsome copper-coloured pimp who controlled four girls in Stamford Hill.

He, Barry and Blake had attended the same school and retained the intimacy of that old link. Blake told his story to Mikey B. when they were alone on the pool table. Mikey B. laughed wildly and asked Blake for the woman's address, saying he might be able to send her some business.

Then Mikey B. became serious, and not for the first time since Barry's illness warned Blake against taking unnecessary risks. They had been burglars together once, when they were younger. But Mikey B. had long abandoned housebreaking. His warning as usual triggered a mild disagreement because Blake resented being lectured to by anyone – except Boswell – and because thieving from houses was a compulsion. He had little control over it. He had returned to the old ways when Barry was hospitalised and knew that the two were connected in some inexplicable way.

Anyway, Blake did not approve of putting women on the street. It was something he and Barry used to talk about and they had both balked at the idea. He now reminded Mikey B. that he, Blake, would never pimp.

'I've told you a million times, Blake,' Mikey B. said, 'I don't pimp. I don't put women on the streets. They pay me to protect them. Go and ask them if I beat them up or rob them. I'm nothing but a glorified security guard, that's all. And now there's some weirdo running around at night scaring the girls, they appreciate me even more.'

'What weirdo?'

'Couple nights back, one of the girls, Helen, came home shaking. Said she'd seen some freak in a ugly mask and straw cape.'

'I've seen it too. Thought I was going crazy,' Blake said, with audible relief in his voice. He described the figure he had seen.

'Whoever he is he'd better watch it, or I'll have to cut him,' Mikey B. said, alluding to the flick knife he always carried, and which, Blake knew, he could use with deadly skill.

When Blake potted the black ball to win a second game, Mikey B. whispered that there was something important he wanted to discuss with him. They went into a far corner where they could talk privately. Mikey B. put a new proposal to Blake. Somebody had offered him half a kilo of top-grade ice; was Blake interested in coming in on a deal?

Mikey B. said: 'The time for hash and weed is past, man. Coke's where the real money is. We could make five or six times our investment.'

Blake was flattered that a top-ranking street hustler like Mikey B. considered him a worthy partner in such a potentially dangerous venture. He felt he was finally emerging from Barry's shadow. He agreed that weed and hash had lost their popularity. There was a time when he could have sold the small bag of hash in his possession within an hour. But Blake was a naturally cautious person. He was loyal too. The weed and hashish had been the mainstay of his livelihood for years. It hadn't made him rich, but he could meet his bills; and he had even managed to save a little money.

He sensed, too, that Mikey B. regarded coke-dealing as a major departure. He, Mikey B., wanted a partner he could trust. Blake did not want to disappoint his friend, so asked for time to think it over.

'It's safe, man, safe,' Mikey B. tried to reassure him. 'Besides, selling a bit of black, breaking into houses – that's for kids, man, Blake. Ice. That's where the real money is. Bet you Barry wouldn't think twice about the deal.'

Blake glowered at Mikey B. and the pimp fell silent. He offered Blake a conciliatory cigarette. They had known each other too long, survived too many scrapes together for the truth to wound too deeply.

When Mikey B. readied to leave, Blake said: 'I hear what you're saying, man. I hear you. Check me tomorrow evening and I'll give you a definite answer.'

Blake left The Hole in search of more customers and other trustworthy listeners to his tale. They were out there somewhere, in the many disreputable haunts that were his world. He belonged to an informal circle of petty thiefs, drug dealers and pimps, men and boys who used a volatile mixture of wit and violence to eke out a precarious livelihood from the gutter of the city. They met daily, unarranged, in the cafés and pubs near their council-estate homes to exchange anecdotes, murder time and give each other support in a perpetual battle against waves of despair. Members distinguished themselves by their sartorial elegance, their pool table skills, their braggadocio. Stars flared and faded in days, hours even, their light extinguished by sudden arrests or romantic distractions or the superior brightness of new stars.

Blake stopped at Granny's Takeaway, where he bought himself a fried dumpling and saltfish sandwich. A mini-cab driver he met there bought a piece of hash off him. From Granny's he headed for the Wellington pub.

The Wellington on weekday afternoons attracted the unemployed, semi-employed and unemployable, wastrels and hustlers of Clapton Estate. It was managed by a thin, jovial St Lucian who was shrewdly myopic to the illicit exchanges of his regular customers. When Blake arrived there he found Kisser George and Knuckles playing a silent game of pool. The friends Blake was expecting were not there. Blake felt the crushing disappointment of a performer discovering, after hours of rehearsal, that he has no audience. Kisser and Knuckles were only fringe members of Blake's circle and both were known for their stolidity and slow-wittedness, the result, according to rumour, of their stint as sparring partners to heavyweight boxers in a local gym. Blake played a game of pool with Knuckles, the smarter of the two dimwits, sold Kisser a piece of hash and moved on in his search for an audience that could appreciate his fantastic story.

The Jerk Pork Café on Sandringham Road finally gave him that audience. T-Bone, Bush, Wire, Matchet, Daddy Irie and Seaga were all there. The circle was like that, constantly shifting its location. For weeks the Wellington would be the meeting place, then The Hole, and then for no reason the Jerk Pork Café. There was much back-slapping and laughter in reaction to Blake's story, and his friends' accounts of other encounters with the masked figure reassured him that he was not going crazy.

By nightfall Blake had sold most of the hash and, satisfied

that he had done a hard day's work, he relaxed. He, Daddy Irie, Matchet and Wire took a cab to Finsbury Park and spent the rest of the evening playing snooker.

Blake got back to Hackney a little before midnight. It had been a good day: he had been a star. He had sold his black and entertained his friends and won their admiration. This made him feel kindly disposed towards the world. He didn't notice the odour of urine in the lift or the smears of excreta on the walls.

His complacency was soon destroyed, though. He assumed that the silence in the flat meant that Sheila had gone to bed early. But when he walked into the living room and switched on the light and saw his blood-stained underclothes stretched across the television he knew otherwise. He had flung them in the bottom of the wardrobe, forgotten about them. He picked up a note from the top of the set and it read: 'I used to wonder what Bloodclawt meant. Now I know. Goodbye.'

Blake slumped into an armchair, rolled a large spliff, and smoked himself into a dreamlike state which numbed his senses and made all the objects of his anxieties – his brother, his mother, Sheila, the woman in Highgate – seem as meaningless as his life.

Chapter Nine

Boswell had not served as the chef since employing Mona; but on this day he decided that Mona's melancholy countenance would be a better sight for arriving customers than his own even sorrier, unshaven appearance. Suddenly his world was in turmoil again. Cleo was back in his life. Rather, Cleo's life was back in his life. If he had read her letter before talking to Stone Mason, he would not have committed himself to the poker game. But it was too late now; he would play his best and leave the rest to the cards. Besides, far more troubling was his deteriorating relationship with Lorette. The scent of betrayed love seemed to grow stronger, more pungent, with each day. He and Lorette had not exchanged more than perfunctory greetings for days. A wide and cold canyon now divided their bed and their nights. Gone were the endearments and little gifts of love; gone were the gentle nocturnal caresses from which he had once drawn strength.

He had long believed that his and Cleo's destinies were somehow intertwined. But a part of him rebelled against the prospect of losing Lorette. She was not Gladstone McDonald's counterpart in his and Cleo's tragic destiny. He was sure of that. Lorette had touched something deep and true and powerful in him. And yet, yet there was that unmistakable odour, as if all the fruits in the world were rotting in one vast vat, the wind scattering their sweet-sour scent of putrefaction. Boswell thought: Every time I think I've found love it turns into a nightmare, this torment.

Maybe I shouldn't have rushed into marriage, he reflected. Maybe I should have got to know her better. He recalled now how they had met in Dougie's nightclub, the instant mutual attraction, the subsequent days they spent in bed, she drinking champagne and he Scotch. Both drunk on that effervescent spring of newly discovered love. She had been divorced for three years and he had not had a steady lover since Carmen, Blake's mother. That affair had ended ignominiously for him, and he had still been nursing the wounds of yet another failure in love. Lorette had taught him how to love again. But what did he really know about her? Only that her brief marriage had ended in tragedy and she was reluctant to talk about it. Yet her dark past had also made her more attractive, more desirable. Then it occurred to Boswell that maybe Lorette had always had a lover, somebody already married, and that he had been drawn into yet another elaborate game of deception. Maybe it's just my imagination, just my crazy love for her, he thought.

Meanwhile, a gang of workmen working on a nearby house entered the Caribbean Sunset Café. They were all black, and their dusty clothes and faces made them look like ghosts. Their entrance roused Mona from her magazine to take their orders. With their raucous laughter and convivial air they suddenly enlivened the Caribbean Sunset Café, dispelling the gloom of rumination and loss that Boswell and Mona created together. These men had nothing more on their minds than food. Or so it seemed at first as they read the menu.

'Rice and peas and chicken,' the eldest of the gang said. The casual authority in his voice, his direct gaze at Mona, which she did not meet, the swiftness of his choice, revealed him to be the leader.

'Don't you ever eat anything else, Winston?' another of the workmen said. He was short and had a round, angelic face and skin the colour of brown breadcrust.

'Yeah, rice and peas and beef; but I'm on a diet,' Winston replied.

They all laughed while Mona, notepad in hand, eyes downcast, shifted about restlessly, nervously.

'Yeah, his missus is complaining,' another member said. He was small and muscular with lively, lascivious eyes and a mischievous smirk. He continued: 'Just when Winston's getting going, she screams, "Ease up, nuh, mahn, ease up! You breaking me ribs." Know what a mean, Frank?' He nudged his workmate seated next to him, and erupted into a laugh which was as infectious as it was salacious.

'Don't you ever think about anything else, Desmond?' Winston said, when he himself had stopped laughing.

'Don't think he does, you know,' Frank said. 'That's cause he can't get it.'

Again they laughed and resumed ordering their lunch. One rice and peas and chicken, one fish and dumpling, two plates of sausages and chips, and cups of tea all round. When Mona left with their orders the men moved to talking about the Dundus.

The week's issue of the local newspaper, the *Hackney Gazette*, had come out that day and it carried a front-page report about a number of strange sightings in the borough. Several residents claimed to have seen a fantastically ugly thing roaming the streets at night. But these eyewitnesses did not agree on its exact appearance. According to a Mr Patrick O'Casey, the chin of its long black face rose out of its chest, its hair consisted of tiny dancing figures, its body was covered in bright golden hair. But another eyewitness, a Leroy Smith, claimed it wore a jewel-encrusted coat; and a Mrs Bridget Jones was quoted as saying it looked like a yeti, monstrously tall with curling tusks, like a wart hog. The report concluded with a quote from the local police chief: 'We have had several calls on this matter from frightened residents over the past month. We believe this is the work of a practical joker. As no crime has been committed we will not be launching an investigation.'

Two of the men knew of people who had met the Dundus and related this to the group. There followed an intense discussion on whether it was really some supernatural being, or the work of a prankster and if so, what was his identity?

The men's excited voices carried into the kitchen, where Boswell was preparing their orders. With one ear cocked in their direction Boswell was momentarily free from his preoccupation with Lorette, Cleo, his failing business and the card game. The loud, carefree laughter of the men in the background as they swapped humorous speculations about the mysterious thing, brought back memories of better days in the Caribbean Sunset Café.

When the orders were ready, Mona brought them to the table. Desmond, who was clearly the clown amongst the gang, had ordered sausages and chips. Mona placed his meal before him and as she did so Desmond said to her: 'Bloody 'ell, these sausages are a bit small. Come and stroke them for me, maybe they'll grow.'

Once again he nudged Frank, who seemed to be the silent serious man of Desmond's comedy act, and burst into a laughter of delight at his own wit.

Mona, who had been jittery in the men's presence, now assumed an expression of mortification and embarrassment.

Winston, the leader, seeing this, said: 'Ignore him, love, he's like this to everybody.'

But it was too late. Mona erupted into tears and turned and fled through a door leading to the toilet.

'Why don't you learn to behave yourself?' Winston said to Desmond fiercely.

Boswell, who had been busy cleaning the surface where he prepared the food, only heard Mona sobbing and saw her back disappear through the door. He quickly went after her, and on finding that she had locked herself in the toilet, her sobbing loud and fitful, he marched back into the café and confronted the diners. 'I don't know what you all did to upset the girl, but if you can't behave yourself then hurry up and eat and don't come back in here until you learn some manners.'

Winston tried to appease him. 'It was a harmless joke,' he said. But Boswell's anger was implacable.

The men hurriedly ate their meals in rueful silence, like children whose pre-meal pranks at the dining table, carried too far, had provoked the wrath of an already troubled mother. Meanwhile, Boswell went to try to persuade Mona to come out. But she would not be moved; her loud sobbing had now become a low, pathetic whimpering.

When the men had paid – with Winston, the leader, still offering profuse apologies – and left, Boswell tried again.

'Come on, Mona, they've gone now. The place is empty. They've gone now.'

At last the door opened and Mona, her eyes red and swollen, her cheeks stained with tears, peered out. On seeing Boswell she threw herself at him and clung to him with a violent desperation, trembling like a delicate leaf in a storm.

'Frigging hell,' Boswell said. He held her reflectively, attempting to comfort her. In the few seconds that they stood there, glued together, Boswell sensed in Mona a distress which went way beyond the immediate incident. It seemed to him that she was suffering from some secret pain, deep and old and unspoken. Her tears soaked through his shirt, chilled the flesh of his chest. But his sympathy was swiftly diluted by an uncontrollable and dangerous desire which he sensed with self-disgust. He clasped Mona's shoulders and firmly peeled her off him. Then in a voice admonishing and full of fear for the dangerous feeling she had aroused, he exhorted: 'Come on, girl, pull yourself together, pull yourself together, they're gone.' He was aware that his admonition was directed at himself as much as her.

She released him reluctantly, allowing her arms to fall limply to her sides, her head lowered, as if in shame, as if in despair. Boswell told her to take the afternoon off, and as soon as she had left, he poured himself a tall drink to steady his nerves.

Soon afterwards Gilbert Singh came rushing into the café, waving a copy of the *Hackney Gazette* in the air and shouting, 'I've seen it, Bosy, I've seen it, too. I've seen the Dundus.'

'Don't be a fool, Gilbert,' Boswell said sternly. 'It's just some damn joker who don't have nothing better to do with his time.'

Despite this harsh response, Boswell was glad to see Gilbert and showed it by offering him a drink. With the lunch hour past, and not a cloud in the sky, the café was unlikely to get any more customers. So the two men settled down to talking. Gilbert gave an account of his encounter with the Dundus and Boswell listened with scepticism and impatience. He was much more interested in Gilbert's racing tips. But Gilbert was too excited about the newspaper report to talk about horseracing. Knowing Gilbert would only get on to that subject once he had exhausted the matter that concerned him, Boswell related the stories he himself had heard about the Dundus.

'Is a bad sign, practical joker or not,' Gilbert said ominously. 'Back home when people start seeing a Dundus, it mean something bad's going to happen, something terrible.'

Those were Gilbert's last words on the matter. He had several tips for Boswell and they spent the next few hours discussing the form of various horses running at Aintree, Epsom and Newmarket over the coming week.

Around closing time, with Gilbert long gone, Boswell was tidying up when he came across the copy of the local paper Gilbert had left behind. It was not a paper that he read but, reluctant to go home, where he was sure that odour would greet him again, he delayed his departure by flicking through the newspaper. In the classified section, his eyes alighted on a boxed advert which read:

IS YOUR WIFE, HUSBAND OR PARTNER
BEING FAITHFUL TO YOU?

IF YOU HAVE DOUBTS, HOWEVER SLIGHT, RING THE
FOLLOWING NUMBER, AND GIVE YOURSELF PEACE
OF MIND. CALL DB PRIVATE DETECTIVE AGENCY
NOW.

Boswell slapped his forehead. Why didn't this occur to me before? he wondered. He jotted down the number and went straight to the telephone.

Chapter Ten

One afternoon Segun Adebayo dropped into the Caribbean
Sunset Café for lunch and found a troubled, careworn-
looking Boswell. The café owner had clearly not shaved in
days and his usually immaculate, if old-fashioned, clothes
bore all the signs of having been slept in; he reeked of whisky
and cigarette smoke. There was no warm, effusive greeting
for the young Nigerian, only a grunted, almost hostile, 'What
can I get you?'

Segun ordered his meal, and when it came ate hurriedly,
while Boswell remained seated behind the counter chain-
smoking. When he went to pay, Boswell looked at him with
strained, bloodshot eyes and said: 'You know what brought
me here, youngman, to this country?'

'No?'

'Love. And you know what keeps me here? Love. So if you
ever want to see your home again, take it from me: don't
look for love.'

Segun was still meditating on that terse, embittered advice
three days later. It was a Saturday night and seated in the
office of AM Cars, waiting for his next assignment, Segun
allowed his mind to play on the sorry sight of the café owner
and his injunction. But a fellow driver, Victor, was distracting
him with more, though not unrelated, advice.

'. . . hell. This city na hell, Segun,' Victor was saying.
Segun's disastrous attempt to rent a room had become
common knowledge amongst his fellow drivers. They had
called him JJC (Johnny Just Come) and taken to lecturing
him on how to survive his new home. He listened in dolorous
silence as Victor, a fellow Yoruba, expatiated on the pitfalls
awaiting unwary newcomers to London. Con artists, Victor
was at pains to stress, were the least of Segun's worries.

'. . . poor Bummi, the immigration officers and police dragged him out of bed. Didn't even give him time to dress properly. But, you know, months later he wrote me from Lagos to say those guys did him a big favour. This London, nawo-o.'

Segun had entered the country on a six-month visitor's visa and was painfully aware that nearly all his time had passed and he was still no closer to finding Sade. He closed his ears to Victor's monologue, and took from his wallet the only photograph of Sade he possessed. It had been taken in Lagos, on Bar Beach. Looking at it revived his determination, raised his hopes.

Sade. Nothing and nobody would prevent him finding her. He recalled their first meeting. He had slept under a palm hut on Bar Beach, the insistent and timeless rhythms of the Atlantic Ocean echoing in his dreams. When the sun prised his eyes open he saw her naked, splashing water on her statuesque body, and he watched in disbelief as the sea cascaded off her, fell like pearls or diamonds. At first he thought he was dreaming, that the sea goddess Yemanja who knew of his loneliness and hunger for a companion had created this wondrous apparition to lure him into her cold and inescapable embrace. When she walked out of the sea towards a pile of clothes he knew he was awake. She donned a short loose linen dress and picked up her shoes and handbag. He stood up suddenly and she was startled. But she quickly composed herself and said: 'Enjoyed the show, Peeping Tom?'

How that feisty voice thrilled him! It resonated with the confidence of a woman who knew that her beauty was her strength. She's probably a bird of the night, he thought. She's probably spent the night in a foreigner's bed. Yet this possibility did not diminish her beauty or appease his desire for her.

Tossing her head like a proud lioness too bored by the size of her prey to continue the chase, she turned and walked away. He shouted after her: 'How can a man be accused of being a Peeping Tom in his own dream?' Her laughter encouraged him, and he snatched up his meagre belongings and ran after her. She allowed him to catch up and though he was an impecunious signpainter and she a bird of the night, that morning, beside the receding but still garrulously loud Atlantic, they discovered each other.

'Zero-five,' the stentorian voice of the controller boomed from behind the glass cage. Victor, who had carried on his rueful monologue unmindful of Segun's disinterest, leapt up. He took instructions from the controller and departed to pick up a passenger in Bethnal Green.

With Victor gone, Segun was alone in the untidy room with its dust-caked carpet, its broken-down chairs where the drivers waited until they were called by the controller. He put the photograph away and his morale sunk again. Slumped in a ragged sofa and perfectly still, he looked like a broken wooden doll. Misery was etched on his handsome face, and his hair, once washed daily, had lost its sheen and was now a flat dull grey. He felt intolerably lonely and as troubled as the ocean on a stormy night. Boswell Anderson's warning, 'Don't let love keep you here,' resounded in his mind like the prophetic utterance of an oracle. He felt as though the Jamaican had read his mind and knew the mission that had brought him to London and could foresee a disastrous ending.

'Zero-nine,' the controller bellowed like a foghorn. Segun Adebayo rose sluggishly from his seat. He stretched and yawned, filling the small room with his long limbs like a tree. He hadn't slept for days and was looking forward to the end of tonight's shift, which would be followed by two days off work.

'Kingsmead Estate. AD ride.'

Segun looked at him through the glass in blank incomprehension.

'AD. As directed,' the controller shouted impatiently. The controller was another Yoruba, with a shaven head and a mountainous stomach which compelled him to sit two feet from the table. Among the drivers it was rumoured that he had been a civil servant in some obscure part of Yorubaland and had amassed a fortune through building contracts and when discovered had fled to London where, poor but alive, he had started AM Cars. Most of the drivers addressed him as the controller, except for the more experienced ones. They sometimes called him chief, an appellation which invariably brought a quivering smile to his pendulous lips.

'Watch how you go in that mad place,' the controller shouted after Segun.

This caution sent Segun reaching into his pocket to check for the talisman he always carried. It was there, a small ball of cotton crisscrossed with black wire. He had bought it from a juju-man before leaving Lagos. It had not prevented any mishaps, but he continued to believe in its protective powers. With his talisman Segun Adebayo feared nothing. Not even Kingsmead Estate on a late Saturday night.

Kingsmead Estate was the least popular pick-up or drop-off point amongst the drivers. Every AM driver had a tale to tell about a Kingsmead ride which had ended in disaster. The most common ruse was for the passenger, on reaching his destination, to leap out of the car and flee without paying. A few drivers had been robbed of their night's takings by knife-wielding youngsters high on crack, low on money and ruthlessly indifferent as to how they financed the next short-lived euphoria. Kingsmead was the short straw; it filled a driver with fear. Following the advice of the more experienced drivers, Segun had ensured that the rear doors on his car were stiff, and the front passenger door required a knack to open it. These precautions, frustrating to the ordinary passenger, helped to give him a sense of security.

He turned into the estate, which faced a stretch of Hackney Marshes, now darkened by the night. The deep thumping bass lines of reggae music filled the air, and for an instant reminded him of the drums which could be heard on a Lagos night issuing from some unseen shrine. Further into the estate, along a brick-paved road which ran between two three-storey blocks, he drove through a curtain of melodic soul music. Then he came to the address. The tension he had been feeling since setting off subsided when he saw a couple waiting at the door of a ground-floor flat. Two men or boys – for they were seldom more than boys – would have put him on red alert. These were obviously party-goers.

The man wore a loose golden-coloured corduroy suit. The

top was like a shirt, with brown pockets. His head was clean-shaven and crisscrossed with patterns. She was dressed in a body-hugging raffia dress of shamelessly short length which exposed muscular knees.

'Bel-Air, first,' the man said. 'Know where that is?'

'Sure,' Segun said.

He reversed out of the estate, the two passengers in the back, and headed towards Stratford. Segun sensed that they had recently argued. They had not said a word to each other since entering the car. The woman, slumped in her seat, simply stared out of the window into the night. From the man came a constant sniffing, as if he had a heavy cold. He was restless, too, changing position every half-minute. When they reached their destination, the man instructed Segun to wait. The woman did not move as the man briskly alighted. He disappeared into the night saying, 'Soon come, babes.' There was no response from her.

Alone in the car with the woman, Segun felt uncomfortable. Her silence was unnerving. He was sure that the couple had quarrelled. The man had probably struck her. What had they quarrelled about? he wondered. Money? That was what most lovers fought about. He remembered a bitter row he had had with Sade. Initially he was indifferent as to how she earned her money. Who was he to pass judgement? He loved her. She could have been one of those spectral figures who moved through the city at night collecting and disposing of shit, he would have still loved her. But it soon became clear that her job exacted a terrible price. Sometimes she showed an insatiable need for reassurances that he loved her. Nobody seeing this beautiful woman dancing her way through the streets of Lagos like a spirit prancing through a forest at dawn would believe the depth of her insecurity. His love for her demanded that he try to change her. That day, the day of their first quarrel, he had tried to dissuade her from haunting the poolside bars of the international hotels where she plied her trade.

It was late afternoon and she had dressed and was ready to leave for her day's work.

'Sade, I don't want you to go to the hotel today,' he said.

'Are you crazy? How we go chop?'

'We have money. Enough to last a month, and I'll find a job soon.'

'Are you crazy? Three hundred naira. That'll be finished by next week. Then what?'

'Not if we spend carefully. One meal a day. Oh, Sade, when you're away at night, I sometimes lie awake thinking of you squashed by some sweating fat foreigner, who just wants to come, and it hurts me to know that's what you're doing just then and your side of the bed is empty and cold.'

'Bed, Segun? Bed? We don't have a bed. You can't call that old bug-ridden mattress that the landlord hauled off the dumpheap a bed. I've never slept in a proper bed of my own, Segun. Always mats on the floor or like that thing. But in the Eko Hotel, now they have beds. Beds so soft you feel that you're floating on the sea. And that's what I want, Segun, a little softness, a little comfort. That's why I go to the Eko or the Sheraton every day. And one day we'll have enough money to stay in those places ourselves.'

'Sade, Sade,' he pleaded, 'we don't need that. We have each other. You and me. I know this room is lousy and infested with all kinds of creepy-crawlies. But it won't always be like this. I'll get a job. My friend Ayo has promised me a break on the newspaper circuit. They make good money, those guys who sell newspapers.'

'Hah, the only people who make money are the journalists, or the men who own them. Selling newspapers.' The ferocity of her indignation enhanced her beauty.

She snatched up her handbag. He threw himself in front of the doorway, aware that his words had failed. 'You're not going anywhere, Sade.'

'Joe! Don't trouble my life,' she said, and tried to push past him.

He grasped her bony shoulder and threw her onto the mattress. 'I told you, you're not going there any more. No more.'

She sprang at him, shouting: 'You don't own me. No man

owns me. You don't even have enough money to buy five minutes of time, Mr Signwriter, Mr Newspaper Vendor, Mr Poorman. Look at you. Who are you?'

Her words were like flaming arrows and they struck their target with accuracy. He gripped her wrists. Her long bony fingers clawed the air as she tried to scratch his face. He struggled with her and was shocked by her strength. Finally he struck her and she reeled backwards and fell on the mattress. She remained holding her face, the face that was her fortune, and sobbing pitifully . . .

'Let's go, man.' His passenger had returned.

'To where?' Segun said.

'Cats, Seventy-Seven, Legends then Dougie's,' he said.

Segun eased the car out, turned it round, and headed back into Hackney. He heard the woman say: 'Get it?'

'Sure, babes. Told you: Mack's my man.'

'How much?'

'Nuff, man. Don't sweat. Nuff.'

After a few minutes of silence, both of them started taking deep breaths, which were followed by sniffing. The man's cold seemed to worsen.

'Good?' he said.

'Brilliant,' she moaned.

Segun's eyes were trained on the road, but all his other senses were tuned in to the couple behind him. He surmised that they were druggies, charlie chasers chasing the night. He had tasted their pleasure many times, when Sade brought some home. Together they had soared above the miserable bare room, above the heat, dust and tumult of Lagos, even above the Atlantic, above the clouds. But that euphoria was always followed by a low which accentuated the squalor and hopelessness of their lives. So one day he refused Sade's white ticket to a temporary heaven, telling her: 'I don't need it. I get high on you,' as he pulled her down onto the louse-infested mattress.

They arrived at Cats, a nightclub beside an all-night petrol station on Homerton High Street. It was now just past midnight and the Saturday night ravers were flocking to the disco.

They arrived in souped-up cars, or new BMWs or battered jalopies. Some of these vehicles were packed with stereos powerful enough to shake the ground. Their occupants poured out in twos and threes, and there was much style in their walk: swaggering shoulders, bouncing steps; and the girls in their tight little black dresses, clutching delicate handbags.

'You coming, babes?' the man said.

'Naw, I'll wait. Try not to be long.'

'Shouldn't be. Just got to make a drop.' He stepped out of the car and merged into a passing group.

Segun was alone in the car with the woman again. She now seemed fidgety in that confined space, and her restlessness distracted him from his preoccupation with Sade. He had not seen her – the woman seated in the back of the car – properly. Her feminine presence had barely registered in his mind up until now. Now it came to him in the scent of her perfume and the possibility of intimacy, and of unburdening of secrets which women always aroused in him.

'You're the quietest cabbie I've driven with,' she said.

He detected in her voice a slightly wounded pride that he had not acknowledged her. Even a perfunctory comment on the weather would have propitiated her need for overt recognition, a subtle need which most men would have sensed earlier and answered.

He laughed lightly and said: 'I'm only the driver.'

A moment of silence passed between them before she spoke again: 'Why are there so many Africans mini-cabbing? Every cab I take these days is driven either by a Nigerian or a Ghanaian. It's as if they have all left their countries to drive cabs.'

'Not all of them,' Segun said. 'Some work in factories.'

'You know what I mean.'

'Why are we here? Is that what you mean?'

'Sort of.'

'To work. Get a share of the Western dream, the same as you West Indians,' Segun said. A half-truth.

'I'm British. A hundred per cent Cockney. I was born in earshot of the great bells of Bow.' She giggled.

The man returned just then, throwing himself into the car, bringing with him the former silence.

'Two more stops, babes, then we can chill out at Dougie's.'

Again Segun drove to the next destination with the couple snorting in the back. At the next stop the man was only away for a short time. But at the next stop, a nightclub in Amhurst Road, she became talkative again.

'So what are you, Nigerian or Ghanaian?'

'Nigerian,' Segun said.

'I know a few Nigerians. Over in Brixton, where I live. There's a flat near me that's full of them. All girls and always having parties. Folake and Sayo, they're the ones. Now there's Sade.'

'Did you say Sade?' Segun said, spinning round in his seat.

'Yeah, Sade. She hasn't been there long; about four months, but she's a scream, like the other two.'

'What does this Sade look like?'

'Oh, I'm useless at describing people.'

'Tall, short, medium? Fat, thin, skinny?'

'Medium height. Well-built. Not fat, though. And very beautiful.'

Segun's heart leapt in his chest and excitement flooded his body. At last a lead, he thought.

'I knew a Sade,' he said. 'I wonder if it's the same person.'

'Maybe. She lives in Macroom House on Coldharbour Lane.'

Before Segun could ask for the exact address the car door opened and the man stepped in. Silence fell.

'To Dougie's,' he said.

Segun sped off towards Dougie's nightclub. It did not bother him that he had no number for the person who might be Sade. Nearly six months ago he had arrived in England believing that she was in Liverpool or London, two big cities, and that had not deterred him. Now, by sheer luck, he had the name of a district and even a sort of address. He could go there as soon as he had finished his shift, sooner if the controller would release him. He would find the building and wait until a decent hour before he started making enquiries.

He was sure he was on the right track. She would be there or somebody there would be able to direct him to her.

The woman did not say anything else on leaving. As soon as she was out of the car, she trotted across the road, her heels echoing on the asphalt. The man remained behind to pay the fare. From his jacket he pulled out an immense bundle of notes, peeled two off and handed them to Segun.

'Nice ride, cabbie. I like a man who knows when to keep quiet.'

Segun took the notes and tucked them away.

Contrary to his wish, the Saturday night became busier. He spent the next two hours ferrying nightclubbers and party-goers around North London. None gave him any trouble. Indeed, he received several handsome tips which made him feel that the gods were finally rewarding him for his prayers, devotions and sacrifices.

Around 4 a.m. Segun got back to the AM office to find three youngmen waiting for a ride. Two were silent and brooding while one played on the game machine. Segun was by now too tired to be alert.

'Stamford Hill for these guys,' the controller said.

They had already paid the controller, a precaution taken for all night rides from the office. Segun led them to his car and they all piled in, two in the back and one in front.

'Cranwich Road,' the front passenger told Segun.

So he set off. But once across the Lea Bridge Roundabout, one of the youngsters demanded that Segun stop so he could relieve himself. Segun pulled the car over as soon as he could, and the passenger got out. But as soon as the boy was out of the car, Segun felt his head pulled back and a powerful arm wrapped around his throat. 'Got him,' a voice said. Next he felt cold steel against his cheek from a knife being held by the front-seat passenger.

'OK, hand it over,' the front-seat passenger said. Simultaneously he reached under the dashboard and started groping. He found a tin of coins which Segun kept for change.

'Fuck, man, is this all you got?'

Segun struggled and the youngster said: 'Cool it, guy, or I'll ram this thing in you.'

There was a calmness about his voice which convinced Segun that the youngman was serious. He thought of the small wad of notes accumulated through the night, of Sade whom he might find in a few hours, of his talisman. He remained still.

'Come on, guy. Where's the rest? Hand it over.'

Segun felt hands pressing against his body, groping, searching hands. Then at last they touched the solid place they had been searching for. The front passenger pulled the wad out of Segun's inner pocket.

'Got it,' he shouted triumphantly.

Just then the youngster who had left the car yanked open the driver's door and shouted: 'Hurry up. There's someone coming.'

Somewhere in the distance the sound of footsteps echoed.

'Let's dig.' The knife clicked shut.

The youths leapt out of the car and ran behind. For the briefest moment Segun was dazed. He rubbed his throat and cheek, feeling the spot where the knife had pricked him. Then he leapt out of the car, saw the direction in which the boys had run and went after them.

A pedestrian subway, seldom used day or night, ran under the Lea Bridge Roundabout, and it was down there that the boys fled. Segun did not hesitate to pursue them; they were only kids, and having survived their assault he was confident he could overpower them.

He flew down the litter-strewn flight of steps and dashed along the half-lit corridor which reeked of urine and beer. He saw one of the boys disappear around a corner. When he reached the corner he found himself hurtling to the ground and his face was suddenly ablaze with pain. Next, feet pummelled his back and his stomach. He curled up like a foetus, trying to protect his head. He heard the boys shouting, 'Cut him, cut him.' He heard a knife click open. Then there was a pause and a voice said: 'Chu, he's had it, mahn. Let's dig up.'

They ran off and in his mind he was giving chase, but there was an excruciating pain in his back and his head was pounding violently and his face felt as though it were on fire. The half-light of the subway was fading, darkening and then becoming brighter again, as if someone were playing with a switch. He tried to stand up, but found himself crawling, gripping the cold concrete floor. The darkness was now almost upon him, and the last sound he heard seemed like footsteps, feminine footsteps, and he thought that maybe Sade had come to rescue him; then the darkness consumed him.

Chapter Eleven

The DB Private Detective Agency was situated above a Turkish grocery store on Stoke Newington High Street. Boswell walked past the shop with its pavement stall of bright and colourful fruit and vegetables several times before summoning the courage to ring the bell on the blue side door. Having closed the Caribbean Sunset Café early, he had travelled by bus to this clandestine rendezvous. As he waited by the door, he made sure his back was turned to the street just in case a passing acquaintance recognised him. This furtive act summed up how he felt about the desperate solution he had chosen to ascertain whether Lorette was having an affair. He was ashamed and afraid. But he had lived with the suspicion for too long. He had to find out.

A cackling male voice issued from the entryphone, demanding his name. He answered and the door clicked open. Climbing the dimly lit stairs in hesitant steps, he thought of abandoning his mission. But when he heard the door above him open, he knew it was too late, far too late to turn back from this course of action which could eventually result in a painful confirmation of his fear, and perhaps the return of the loneliness he had not known since Cleo's departure.

He was met on the landing of the second floor by a short stout man with an oily forehead and small dark eyes set in a pleasantly reassuring face.

'Ah, Mr Anderson, come in. My name's Darius Benedict. I've been expecting you.' He extended a hand and Boswell shook it with reluctance.

Boswell followed him into a room which overlooked the High Street. The evening light filtered through dirty windows and diffused below a humming fluorescent bulb, which covered the width of the high ceiling. Two Edwardian mahogany screens divided the room, and in the narrow space between them Boswell could make out a bed and wash basin. On seeing these signs of a home, Boswell regretted that he hadn't called off this distasteful project while he had the chance. The rest of the room was no more inspiring. A small desk, two rusting filing cabinets of inestimable antiquity, and in front of the desk two cloth-covered upright office chairs which looked as if they had been rescued from a rubbish tip; they were caked and shiny with dirt. It was the office and home of a man on the brink of destitution.

'Do sit down, Mr Anderson.' Benedict pointed to one of the dirt-encrusted chairs. He took a seat behind the desk, on a handsome Georgian captain's chair, the one redeeming piece of furniture.

'Now what can we do for you, Mr Anderson?' Benedict said. There was hint of the Eastern Caribbean in his voice, Trinidad or Barbados or Guyana.

Boswell, so articulate in his own domain, so confident, now fumbled for words in the squalid office-cum-home of the private detective. His embarrassment rendered him incoherent.

'Say no more, Mr Anderson.' Mr Benedict stopped him with the knowingness of a man who had heard a thousand similar stories. 'You believe your wife's having an affair.'

'In short, yes,' said Boswell. There, it's out, he thought. And he was flooded with relief and gratitude for Benedict's quick understanding, without him having to mention what would have probably seemed like absurdly flimsy grounds for his suspicion.

'You're embarrassed, Mr Anderson. Don't be. Adultery is the most common case we deal with. Or rather alleged adultery. We don't know yet in your case whether she's guilty. But we can soon find out. It will cost you, though.'

'How much?'

'I usually spend a month on a case. One hundred pounds a week, plus the same again for expenses.'

'That's eight hundred pounds,' Boswell said, alarmed, as he deducted the sum from the funds he was trying to accumulate for the poker game. If he hired Benedict he would have to withdraw.

'You don't have to hire me, Mr Anderson. You can go to any number of agencies. Plenty listed in the Yellow Pages. I think you'll find that my rate is very competitive. Or maybe you want to leave things as they are. And I bet I know how things are, Mr Anderson. You're probably not sleeping at night. You've probably lost your appetite, lost weight, can't concentrate on anything. Every minute you spend away from her you're wondering who she's with. Vivid pictures of some man, some stranger, loving up your wife play day and night. Soon, if you haven't started already, you'll be seeing her lover in the face of every man who looks at her, your best friend, your brother even. You probably haven't touched her since the suspicion took root, and now it's a monstrous serpent strangling all desire you had for her. Am I wrong, Mr Anderson? Am I wrong or right?'

'I haven't got a brother,' Boswell said petulantly.

Benedict laughed drily and sat down again.

'You're right,' Boswell said, 'this thing's become an obsession.'

'Of course I'm right, Mr Anderson.' Benedict leant across the desk. 'I've been in this business for twenty years. So I know exactly what you're going through. Let's face it, Mr Anderson,' Benedict said, standing, resting his fingers on the desk, 'you ain't the first, and you won't be the last man to suspect his wife of tomfoolery. You think when the bible talks of Eve eating the apple given her by the serpent it meant the apple literally? No, mahn. Is about Eve going off into the bush with another man. And don't think Adam was a saint. You see, Mr Anderson, marriage is an unnatural state. We're on this earth to procreate, to multiply. Is a biological thing. Fidelity is impossible, except amongst people with a low sex drive . . .'

'Alright, alright,' Boswell said. He was not there for a philosophical lecture on the impossibility of marriage. 'Look, I just want you to find out if she has another man. That's all.'

'Sorry to lecture you, Mr Anderson. But you see, with my

years of experience I know how much courage it takes to come here, face a complete stranger with that kind of information. Some men lose courage at this point, right where you're sitting. Call the whole thing off, and go back to a life of endless torment until they die of a heart attack or cancer or they beat up the woman so bad they end up in prison. Worse thing is, though, sometimes the affair is just in their imagination.'

'I hope it's just my imagination,' Boswell said.

'For your sake and her sake I hope so too. Now that will be half the fee to start the job. And the rest at the end of the four weeks.'

'And what do I get for this money?'

'A weekly report detailing her every movement outside the house and who comes a-calling in the day. And peace of mind, peace of mind.'

'Eight hundred pounds. A lot of money,' Boswell said, glancing around the room. Benedict's confidence had helped to assuage his misgivings about spying on Lorette, but Boswell the businessman and prospective gambler in a high-stake poker game was reluctant to part with such a large sum of money. Exploiting his own genuine doubts, Boswell appeared to be having second thoughts.

Benedict's professional certainty suddenly collapsed. 'Well, maybe I can give you a discount.'

Boswell leapt at this possible concession, and negotiated a reduced fee. But Benedict had relented so quickly that Boswell became curious. He said: 'How long did you say you been in this business?'

'Er, ten years,' Benedict said, hesitantly.

'Strange, I've been living round here for over twenty years, ain't come across you or the DB Private Detective Agency.'

Benedict's pretence collapsed under Boswell's probing, sceptical gaze. 'Alright, alright, I've been going for about a month now. Give me a break, mahn. I know what I am doing. I've read all the manuals.'

Boswell smiled wryly and said: 'We've made a deal, Mr

Benedict. I'm not going to back out. I just don't want you thinking you're dealing with a fool.'

'No, no, I wouldn't think that. But you know most people are impressed when you tell them you been around a while. Makes them feel safe with you.' Benedict looked sheepish, unlike the confident, philosophising detective he'd appeared to be moments before.

Boswell did not press home his advantage any further. Having toppled Benedict from his professional pedestal, he relaxed and said in an incredulous, conversational tone: 'What made you go into this business, anyway?'

Benedict became less ill at ease, smiled and said: 'You been hearing these stories 'bout the Dundus?'

'Yes, in the pub, from friends. Even read about it in the paper, same paper where I found your number.'

'Well, where I come from, Mr Anderson, when people start seeing the Dundus it usually means trouble, trouble for married couples, for lovers. Plenty broken hearts. Few weeks back, after three people told me about it, being a man who's always looking for the main chance, though I ain't found it yet, I got the idea of starting this agency.'

'This Dundus business, seems I just can't get away from it.'

'You know the story 'bout the Dundus, how it came in to being?'

'Was probably told as a kid, back in Jamaica, but I can't say I do now.'

'Well, every island's probably got their own account. But our own – I come from a little place called Aruba, near Grenada – goes something like this. Many years ago, there lived a very rich woman who was versed in the secret arts. She lived in a splendid mansion on top of a hill, and peacocks roamed its grounds. This woman was feared for miles around because she had supposedly gained her wealth by poisoning her husband, and to ensure that she kept that wealth, visitors were discouraged from calling at the house. Her sole companion was a stunningly beautiful girl she had adopted as a baby. The girl was called Soledad and no man had ever set eyes on her without weeping at her beauty and her inaccessibility. So the legend goes.

'Then one day, into the village came a youngman, brash and scornful of the villagers' superstitious ways. By and by, he saw Soledad roaming the mansion grounds, the peacocks feeding from her hands. Well, that was it. He was in love. The villagers warned him to keep away. But you know youngmen: they believe the world is theirs to conquer and will recklessly follow their hearts. So this youngman started wooing Soledad. By and by, they began to meet beside the sea, late at night, early morning, where the youngman would inflame her heart with poetry and wondrous tales of the city where he came from. The stepmother found out, tried to prevent Soledad from seeing her lover again. But it was too late. Soledad was hopelessly in love. Then disaster struck. One day, returning from a tryst with her lover, still intoxicated by his kisses and caresses, the girl slipped and fell. In another version I have heard, vultures swooped out of the sky and pecked out her eyes. To cut a long story short, she lost her sight. Later, the stepmother brought the blinded Soledad to the youngman's quarters. When our lover boy saw Soledad, her eyes bandaged, her clothes bloodied, he took flight and ran away to the highest peak on the island, where he died mourning the love he had betrayed.

'The Dundus, people say, is his spirit, and whenever it comes it means trouble for lovers.'

Boswell frowned, not in scepticism, but because he did not recognise the story. 'Well, I think is some joker.'

'Doesn't matter, Mr Anderson. You know why I believe that? A few years before I set off for England, some foolish masquerader decided that he was going to play the Dundus at that year's carnival. I wouldn't like to tell you the amount of divorces that followed. My parents, even the Governor. His wife found him *in flagrante delicto* with the housekeeper. She packed her bags and left the island. Maybe it is somebody playing a joke but he don't know what he's joking with. Is a serious t'ing.'

'And you're going to make a profit from it?'

'You sound like a businessman, Mr Anderson. Do you blame me?'

Boswell shook his head and was suddenly filled with an urgent need to get away from Benedict's office. He finalised their agreement in brisk, businesslike manner. He gave Benedict his home address and described Lorette. Given a choice between collecting the weekly report from the detective's office or having it delivered at some prearranged location, he chose the latter. Although he was now fully committed to hiring Benedict, there was no need for the whole world to know. He also agreed to bring half the fee the following day – a particularly painful aspect of the deal.

As they shook hands in parting, Benedict, his professionally reassuring tone restored, said: 'You won't regret hiring me, Mr Anderson. Whatever the outcome.'

'We'll see,' Boswell said, and hastily made his way out of the building.

As he walked along Stoke Newington High Street, now crowded with people making their way home, the sharp ring of shutters closing, the hum and purr of car engines stuck in the traffic jam, Boswell felt wretched and unclean. Every hundred yards, he stopped to look at his reflection in a shop window. Each time he saw the tall figure with its hunched shoulders, brown suit and melancholy face beneath a trilby hat he thought he saw a reprehensible stranger. And he would mutter to the glass: 'So this is what your life has come to, Boswell Anderson, spying on your wife.' Standing outside the window of a furniture store, it occurred to him that if Lorette was being unfaithful he would have no choice but to leave her. This realisation was immediately followed by searing memories of empty, lonely evenings and unending, desolate nights when even alcohol couldn't purchase him oblivion, respite from the torment of solitude. Before Lorette – the years with Cleo and Carmen apart – he had felt bereft and in need of the comfort of a companion even when he was surrounded by friends. But those friends, who did once help him make it through many vacant, loveless days, were a dwindling band, heading back home. How would he survive the future that the present threatened? Oh, Lorette, let it be my imagination, he thought, let it be this crazy love, and I'll tame it and rescue you from me, and me from myself.

Chapter Twelve

Blake was seated opposite his mother, Carmen, as the train pulled out of Liverpool Street station. Their destination was Gospen Park, an hour's journey from London. They had been making this fortnightly trip to visit Barry for almost a year, but Blake still found it an ordeal. It wasn't just what awaited them at the other end, the uncertainty whether Barry would recognise them, his seemingly incurable dementia, his pathetic state. It was also Blake's tormented relationship with his mother.

This journey had started well. Carmen had attended a party the previous night and the gaiety of the occasion was still in her eyes and stained her smile. She was in a nervously talkative mood. The price of goods in the market, her noisy neighbours, the storylines in *EastEnders*, friends she had recently met, fragments of memories from her childhood. Blake saw in her garrulity a familiar ploy to keep her mind off their destination and Barry, but welcomed this change from the almost funereal silence that had hung over recent trips.

Unfortunately, as soon as the train pulled out of the station, Carmen's liveliness vanished. Mother and son sat opposite each other in the near-empty carriage, gazing out of the window, avoiding eye contact like two people who shared a shameful secret.

Carmen Matthews had a light brown complexion and fine features, which in her youth had given her such an exotic appearance that East Londoners had often described her, with admiration, as an Ethiopian. In fact, her roots extended deep into the Essex marshes through her mother. A lonely and deprived childhood with her alcoholic English mother – who could tell her nothing about her father except that he was a dark-skinned sailor – teenage motherhood, years of hardship bringing up two boys, and innumerable failed romances had aged her prematurely. Only her large, lively brown eyes contained any traces of youth. And nowadays nobody mistook her for an Ethiopian.

The train gathered speed through the ultimate back streets of the city, where night dumpers abandoned broken prams and beds and sundry pieces of furniture on the slopes above the tracks, and Blake tapped out on the table the rhythm of a frustration that was deep and old and inexpressible. He had been seeking, with mute desperation, his mother's attention all his life. But Carmen's maternal nourishment was reserved only for Barry.

Carmen's attitude predated Barry's illness: Barry had always been a wall between Blake and Carmen. Born within minutes of each other, with Barry emerging first, the twins early on revealed radically different temperaments. Blake was quiet and slept a lot. Barry was a difficult baby. He screamed and cried for food, for attention, for relief from discomfort. Every night for two years Carmen stayed up with him to prevent his loud incessant bawling, which Blake somehow always slept through, and which defied all soporific concoctions. In their first five years Carmen's life revolved around keeping Barry alive. He survived those early perilous years and each day grew to resemble his absent father, Apollo Matthews, otherwise known as The Bird.

Apollo Matthews was a dancer and sweetman whom Carmen, an innocent teenager, had met in the Casablanca Club on the Old Kent Road. His sweet promises to take her to an island of perennial flowers, ubiquitous greenery and constantly warm sunny days interrupted by star-spangled nights or the dulcet music of the rain, those sweet promises fatally enchanted her. Their year together filled her with a violent dissatisfaction with her life in Canning Town. Only the complications in her pregnancy prevented her from leaving when Apollo suddenly disappeared shortly after learning of his imminent fatherhood. Apollo's flight confirmed what her misanthropic mother always said: 'God made woman from the rib of man but it was the rib contained the power to love. So men can't love. All they do is fuck and run.'

When the boys were three, Carmen heard from Apollo. He wanted her to join him in Hackney. Ignoring her mother's warnings, she joined him. They married and lived in one room in Stoke Newington. On Saturday nights they would visit the Caribbean Sunset Café where everybody knew Apollo as The Bird, because his dancing feet were as fast as the beating wings of a hummingbird and on an exceptional night he could achieve a six-inch levitation off the ground for about thirty seconds.

By the age of ten Barry bore a striking resemblance to Apollo Matthews. And like his errant father, Barry demanded attention. The boy seemed to be possessed by a demon. He was constantly in trouble at school, fighting, playing truant, swearing at teachers. He and Blake were similarly tall and rangy. But Barry carried himself with a precocious self-assurance long after Blake was still struggling to come to terms with his body and shed the gauche gait of a teenager who had suddenly shot up in height. Barry's precocity kept alive Carmen's dream of escape implanted in her mind by Apollo. Barry was to be her redeemer. It was a role he arrogated to himself and which she foisted on him. He bristled with energy, had a sharp wit, abundant imagination and exuded an effortless charm.

When Barry beamed his smile on Carmen she felt as if she had been blessed by some benevolent being in transit through her world of dereliction. One of Carmen's greatest pleasures was to be seen walking down the street with Barry, close, their arms linked, and she would imagine that he was Apollo Matthews and all the women they passed were envious of the strikingly handsome youngman in her company.

Yet Carmen loved Blake no less than Barry. But she loved him through Barry and not for himself. Initially, she mistook Blake's quietness and detachment for timidity. Later she came to recognise that Blake possessed an evenness of temper which – though it made him seem dull and unimaginative – served as a rein on Barry's wilder temperament. So she came to rely on Blake for Barry's survival. Barry was expected to misbehave, to go to extremes, and Blake was supposed to be the brakes.

When Barry began to accumulate a string of minor criminal convictions, she appealed to Blake to control his brother, and berated him for failing to do so. Consequently Blake felt that a part of Carmen blamed him for Barry's illness, as if it were a misdemeanour that Blake should have checked. He feared that perhaps in a deep and dark recess of her heart she wished that it was he and not Barry who had fallen victim to that swift and inexplicable malady.

The train stopped in Gospen, a small bleak windswept station served by a single low-hung ancient Cortina driven by a silent middle-aged man who had taken them to Gospen Park on previous visits.

Gospen Park began with a long wall overhung with ivy. A security guard manned its tall black iron gate. They were driven through it and along a narrow driveway lined with miniature fir trees that were immaculately trimmed, like the surrounding lawn. They alighted outside the main building, a neo-gothic structure of Bath stone and redbrick.

They were led down a long, wide corridor of polished wooden tiles smelling of disinfectant. At the end of the corridor was a modern extension of the building, where the corridor narrowed, and the ceiling became lower.

Barry was sitting at the far window of this communal room. Two patients played table tennis and others sat around reading, talking or staring into space.

'You've got visitors, Barry,' the nurse chirped.

He did not respond. It was as though he had not heard. He continued gazing through the window, at the dark green landscaped garden which rolled down to a distant pond.

Blake said: 'Hey, B. Mummy's here as well.'

Barry turned round slowly and looked at them with vacant eyes set in an ashy face of immense balloon cheeks. He raised a hand of bulbous fingers and touched his cheeks. He had recognised them.

The nurse said: 'I'll leave you then. You can take him for

a walk if you like. He likes that. Walking. He's been very good. Haven't you, Barry?'

Blake and Carmen guided Barry outside. They walked to the pond, with Blake talking nonstop in an effort to reach Barry, to pull him back from whatever barren wilderness he now dwelt in. When they reached the pond, Carmen took over and attempted to stir childhood memories of autumn Sunday afternoons collecting conkers in Victoria Park, or rare summer holidays beside the sea, of his first bicycle. Barry shuffled between them, a silent pitiable figure who would not be recognised by even the most ardent admirers in his former life.

They had circled the small stagnant pond without receiving any sign from Barry that he understood them. Suddenly he stopped and his gelatinous face seemed to acquire a mask of intense concentration, as though he were listening for a faint far-off sound. Blake then noticed the growing damp at the front of his brother's trousers.

Blake and Carmen linked arms with Barry and steered him back into the building. Here a nurse took him away, and he was brought back with a change of clothes. They ate lunch together and afterwards sat in the common room overlooking the landscaped garden. Then it was time to leave because Barry had to have his medication and his afternoon nap. Carmen hugged him, and kissed his cheek but she might as well have been saying goodbye to an inanimate object. Blake lifted his brother's hand, shook it, and on release it fell back to his side lifelessly. Then Barry followed the nurse like a dumb obedient child, shuffled beside her down the long corridor.

Back on the train, the effects of the three-hour visit were visible on Carmen's face. She was exhausted: her face was drawn, films of tears clouded her reddened eyes.

Blake watched his mother fighting off sleep and continued watching her when she began to doze. Disconsolation worsened his own emotional fatigue, denied him the temporary forgetfulness of sleep. Contrary to Boswell's advice, the monster troubling him would not disappear if he closed his eyes. It dwelt in his heart. He desperately wanted his mother to recognise him as a person in his own right, not an appendage to Barry. But the harder he struggled to find the words to express this heartfelt desire, the further he retreated into himself. Words. Barry had been the one with words and the courage to use them. He had never been afraid to voice his own fears and desires and anxieties. If Blake could have found those words which once came so easily to Barry, maybe he could have reassured Carmen that Barry would recover, become his old self again. If he had words he would let Carmen know that until that day and for ever he would protect and love her like the son he was, if she would give him the chance. He was not Barry, poor Barry; he couldn't make her laugh with a grimace of his face, or some outrageously funny joke; clothes just did not hang on him the same way; he couldn't look like Apollo Matthews, but he wanted and needed the same love she had poured on Barry all those years, that love that he had had to scramble for like an indigent uninvited guest scrambling for crumbs from the cake of love that she gave so generously to her favourite son.

At Liverpool Street station, Blake saw his mother into a taxi. Through the open window he said: 'Barry'll come round, Mummy. It's just a matter of time.' She looked straight into his eyes as if probing for insincerity, as if searching there for some reason why she should make another visit, and said, 'Oh God, Blake, I hope so. I hope so.'

Late that night Blake drove to Highgate and parked outside the house he had burgled some weeks before. There were no signs of life inside, but he remained in the car, eyes trained on the house, his mind in turmoil, struggling with feelings for which he had no words.

Chapter Thirteen

Lorette hurried through the flat, closing the curtains, shutting out the weak afternoon light. She was expecting a visitor who disliked the light; only semi-darkness would ensure his presence.

When she finished she returned to the hallway for the shopping bags she had dropped there after rushing home from Ridley Road market. It was there, while trying to decide what to buy for dinner, that she had received his message. She put away the plantains, tins of ackee and packets of saltfish; then she ran the bath. She poured into it liberal drops of foxglove oil and extract of pimento flowers, which an aunt had sent from Jamaica.

Leaving the bath to fill, she went back to the darkened bedroom and turned face down the framed photograph of her and Boswell on their wedding day. Then she undressed and wrapped her body in the purple silk kimono. How she loved the feel of silk against her skin, so fine, so smooth, like being clothed in a light breeze, like walking naked in a tropical drizzle, like his fingers stroking her. He also adored silk: the kimono was a gift from him. She faced the wardrobe mirror and gazed at her reflection indulgently. Despite her greying hair, her loosening muscles, he still worshipped her body. Just as he said he always would.

As if in a trance she walked slowly from the bedroom into the bathroom, and turned off the water. She hung the kimono on the door and stepped into the steaming aromatic water. She immersed herself in it and felt the oils seep into her skin. Once her visitor had arrived while she was still in the bath and he had joined her there. Though the bath was far too small for two adults, she had enjoyed having his weight on her with the hot, oily water lapping her body. But she had protested afterwards and since then he only came to her in the bedroom. But this hot bath, like the closed curtains, was still necessary.

Lorette closed her eyes and rested her head on the cushion at the back of the bath. The combination of hot water and oils was soporific, but she resisted drowsing off because even the briefest nap would puff up the skin below her eyes. She did not like him to see her like that; she had to look her best for him. She wondered what he would wear today: would he be dressed in his tuxedo, looking formal and severe; or would he wear casuals?

Now she concentrated on him, on her memory of him. She allowed herself to remember, floated back to those dismal years before he entered her life. How young and foolish she was then. Every nightclub owner in Soho had used and abused her. They had promised her stardom and wealth and love. The price, a night with her. How desperate and blind she had been. Deaf as well. For her voice was never really up to scratch. It took her many years to recognise that painful truth, and as many years to resign herself to it. It was a pleasant voice. Nothing more. Had she been less blessed with good looks she might have discovered her shortcoming earlier in life. She might not have defied her father's wishes that she become a schoolteacher, she might not have been seduced by the pictures of glamorous Black American singers which decorated the album sleeves of her parents' small record collection. But the knowledge of the limit of her talent came late. It happened when one morning she woke up in the bed of Frank Wright, the obese manager of the Cotton Club in Dean Street, and overheard him say on the telephone: 'Nah, she can't sing for toffee. But what a body, my God, what a body. Like eating a big chocolate cake all to yourself. OK, OK, I've only booked her for a week. Her stint finishes in two days. Alright, Mr Hawkes, she'll be gone by then.' She had guessed that he was talking to the club's owner.

She did not go back to the Cotton Club that night or ever. She swore to give up singing, and rented a bedsit in Bayswater. It was there that she met him. He lived upstairs and played keyboards in recording sessions. She sang for him and when he heard her voice he immediately said they should team up, become a duo. He revived her youthful dreams, restored her confidence, rescued her from the scrapheap of defeat and banished the depression that had transformed her into a hermit.

She saw him clearly now, saw Oscar, her late husband, seated at the baby grand piano in the apartment where they last lived together. He was deep in practice and seemed unaware of her presence. She called his name . . .

Suddenly there was a knock on the front door and Lorette started.

'Who's that?' she shouted.

'Pest control, ma'am,' a squeaky male voice returned.

Lorette cursed softly, got out of the bath, wrapped a towel robe around herself, and put on her kimono. Pest control! She wiped off the perspiration which the hot steam bath had caused and went to the door. Remembering Boswell's advice not to answer the door without the chain lock being on, she ensured that it was, then she opened the door slightly.

She saw a strange little man in blue overalls, matching peaked cap and thick convex glasses. He held a clipboard, and as soon as he saw her he flashed an official-looking card in her face. It read: 'Harold Smith, Pest Inspector, Hackney Council.' It was embossed with a photograph of the little man's peculiarly disturbing face. She did not for one moment doubt its authenticity, but she was still cautious.

'What do you want?'

'We notified you a week ago that we'd be inspecting these flats. Several tenants have reported an invasion of cockroaches. It's the heating vents, you know. They breed them. Terrible.'

She could not recall seeing any notification. It occurred to her that perhaps Boswell had seen the letter and forgotten to tell her. Whatever the case, she did not want this stranger in her home. 'We're OK. There aren't any cockroaches in here.'

'That's what you think, ma'am. Those little buggers are clever. They know just where to hide. Our department have identified a superintelligent breed resistant to the chemicals and devilishly clever. Of course they reveal themselves eventually. But if we can get to them before that time, while they're still young, we can get rid of them easier. An inspection only takes ten minutes.'

He had persuaded her. She unhooked the chain and allowed Harold Smith entry. He went straight to the kitchen and began opening cupboards and shining a torch into dark inaccessible corners. He unscrewed a heating vent and stuck his head into it – at one point almost half his body. He went through the bathroom, the living room, where he lifted up the sofas and chairs, and disturbed the records. Next he searched the bedroom, looking into the wardrobes and under the bed.

'Common breeding ground, under the bed,' he said. 'Not many people know that. Get into the mattress, nice and warm and soft, lovely for them cockroaches.'

Lorette felt that this Harold Smith was teasing her. It was an inexplicable feeling, something about those thick glasses and his wry smile. But more than anything she was annoyed. He had swept through her home, probing and poking into its dark recesses and most private nooks like a bug-eyed spy. She watched him with a mounting sense of outrage and indignation and impatience. For she longed to get back into the bath and feared that Harold Smith's interruption had frightened her visitor away, had broken the spell that he answered to. Arms folded, she half-listened to the intruder's running commentary on his exploration into the hitherto undisturbed crannies of her life, and half implored Oscar to continue his journey to her. This nuisance would soon be gone.

'All clear. That's it.'

'I told you, Mr Smith,' she said.

'No sign of those little devils. But better safe than sorry, as they say.'

Lorette walked to the corridor and Harold Smith followed her. There he dusted off the knees of his blue overalls. Watching him, Lorette thought what a strange little man. She wondered whether people who had followed the occupation for many years soon came to resemble the creatures they dealt with. For there was definitely something insect-like about Harold Smith.

'Bet you's a Jamaican,' Mr Smith said. They were standing in the doorway.

'That's obvious,' she said.

'Not really. It's not in your accent. Couldn't place you at first.'

'So what gave me away?'

'I know my own people.'

She smiled patronisingly: 'Good for you, Mr Smith.'

On another occasion she might have asked him which parish or district he came from. But she was too anxious to see him gone to exchange notes on Jamaica.

'Clean as a whistle. Won't have to send the terminators to your flat. Others aren't so lucky, you know. Overrun with them they are.'

'Thank you, Mr Smith, thank you.'

She closed the door firmly, without banging it, and put the chain on. Through the frosted glass she could still see the diminutive figure of the pest inspector. Why was he lingering there? Anyway, he was out of her home; that was the important thing.

She hastened back to the bath, which was now lukewarm. So she drained some off and ran more hot water while lying in it. When the temperature had reached its former height, she shut her eyes tightly and called to him: 'You can come now. I'm alone again.' The minutes ticked by and there was no sign of his presence. He had turned back, deterred by the interloper. Silently, she pleaded, exhorted and promised him all sorts of new pleasures if he came. At last she felt his presence approaching. Gradually, like a photograph developing, the figure at the piano began to reappear. It would be a while before he arrived fully but she knew now that he had halted his retreat, that they would soon be together again.

Lorette rose from the bath, dried herself, and put on the purple kimono. In a daze, she walked to the bedroom. There she oiled herself with extract of hibiscus and then tied up her hair in a red and yellow band. Then she lay on the bed, lay perfectly still with her eyes shut.

Once again the memories came flooding back. This time they were warm memories of the lean months when neither earned a penny and they lived off cornmeal porridge and boiled cabbage and if it was winter they stayed in bed all day to save fuel. And she remembered too the autumn days when they strolled through Hyde Park holding hands, golden leaves falling around them, brief moments when they seemed to be the only people for miles around. Lying there she relived that intense feeling of togetherness, being at one with him, so completely and indissolubly linked that his heartbeat was her own, the rhythm of his breathing moved her breast. 'Come to me, my love, my love, come to me,' she moaned whisperingly.

She heard the gentle knock that he always gave. She whispered, 'Come in.'

'I thought you'd changed your mind,' she said. She was pleased that he was wearing his tuxedo, a sign that he had made a special effort to appear presentable for her.

'There was someone here. I couldn't come earlier.'

He strolled to the bed and laid down beside her. She undressed him and together they lay naked on the bed, now encoiled, now apart, always touching, though. The anxiety caused by the interruption had drained her. But he was understanding; he did not press her to make love. Instead he kneaded her back with his strong soft fingers, the fingers of a piano player. He ignored her solicitude for his hands. He said he was not playing that evening: 'So let me play music on your body, my love.' Sweet words, words that dizzied her. She would never, never tire of being played by him.

When her visitor had departed, when the spell had been broken, when she reawakened, she remained on the bed and wept in remorse and confusion. She picked up the wedding photograph, held it against her breast, and sobbed: 'I'm sorry, Bosy. I'm sorry. I didn't mean to start this again. But I can't help it. I can't. Help me, Boswell, please help me.' If only you would fight, Boswell, she thought. I thought you were made of sterner stuff, greater resilience. Fight and he'll go away. Oh, Boswell, dear, dear Boswell. I'm losing you, just as I've lost so many lovers over the years. I don't want to lose you, Boswell. But I'm powerless in the face of something far, far stronger. Even as I mourn the passing of what we once shared, Boswell, I'm looking forward to his next visit.

By early evening Lorette's confused ambivalence had passed. She no longer doubted her love for Boswell. She decided to prepare a special meal for him over which she would remind him of what had brought them together at this late hour in their lives. Neither dreamt of returning to the Caribbean, and both feared loneliness in old age. She would reveal the secret of her afternoon ritual, seek his help in bringing it to an end, for her sake, for his sake, for their future happiness. She would make him recognise that her love needed more than gifts and outbursts of jealousy. She did not want gestures of affection. He had to devote more time to her and less to the Caribbean Sunset Café. If he had to continue running that failed, outdated business, then once he arrived home he had to put it out of his mind and be with her in body, heart and soul. His erratic and seemingly distracted love was not good enough.

Lorette's meal, prepared with all the love of her troubled heart, went uneaten that evening. Boswell staggered in after midnight, reeking of whisky, and fell asleep in the living room. She left him there and went to bed, frustrated and disgusted. Early the next morning she was awoken by the sound of the front door banging shut as Boswell departed for the Caribbean Sunset Café, the rival that had driven her to exhume the ambiguous memory of her late husband.

Chapter Fourteen

On the last morning of her short life Mona Xavier, with eyes that were sadder than a rainy Sunday morning, watched Vincent pass by. Vincent lived a few houses away and there was a time when she used to dream that he would rescue her from her prison of silent misery, scale the walls and magically transport her to everlasting happiness on a mountainous green island crisscrossed by rivers that tumbled over immense white boulders. The island was part of her past, but Vincent, a scholarly and rather self-absorbed youngman, would never be part of her future.

Mona had not always been so unhappy. When she first came back to London from Dominica, where she had been sent at the age of five, she seemed like a perfectly average twelve-year-old. She was a little shy, but had a radiant smile. One day at school a cruel punster called her Monkey Lisa from Dominica. She bloodied his nose in a fight that was talked about for weeks afterwards. Having betrayed that she was easily provoked, she became the object of other cruel names. She fought every day. The teachers urged Mona to be less sensitive to name-calling; they were harmless jokes. So Mona became less sensitive. She willed herself to grow an unbreachable shield, and withdrew until the only voice she heard was her own. Within a few years she became a lonely withdrawn teenager who each evening trudged home from school, her uniform and hair dishevelled, her steps slow and heavy, as if she were climbing an interminable mountain path in the raging heat of a Caribbean afternoon.

Before her father found her the job at the Caribbean Sunset Café, she had been sacked for incompetence by all the major stores in Hackney, and the canteens of a local hospital and a college.

Deep down inside, Mona wanted to be back in Dominica. She had been happy living with Granny Celeste Xavier, and had never recovered from the separation. Granny Celeste and Vincent used to figure nightly in her dreams. But recently Celeste had become the sole inhabitant of that verdant landscape that survived in her memory and came vividly alive at night.

One dream in particular recurred regularly. Following her grandmother's instructions she plants a mango seed beside the red wooden house where she lives. It sprouts and she tends it with loving devotion. She shades it against the severe heat of the sun, shelters it from heavy rainfalls, measures its height daily with a ruler. Every day she asks Granny Celeste if the sapling will really grow as tall and wide as other mango trees and bear fruit. Granny Celeste laughs and says, 'If you give it enough love.' Then one afternoon she returns from school to find the sapling lying on the ground, uprooted and withered. She bursts into tears and replaces the tender young plant into the ground and waters it with those tears and it becomes strong again. This recurs countless times until one day her tears are exhausted and the plant dies.

That Saturday of her own death, after watching Vincent pass below from her bedroom window on the top floor of her parents' home, Mona Xavier tidied her room and then resumed her vigil. She was hoping to see Vincent again but all she saw was the street come alive as women made their way to the market for the week's shopping. She saw her own mother leave the house and watched until she disappeared.

Around mid-morning she saw her eldest brother, Eddie, drive up in his green sports car. He was wearing a brown check jacket and blue jeans and there was a large round brass buckle on his belt. He took from the car a box and carried it ceremoniously towards the house. A gift for his mother. She heard him enter and some minutes later Mona thought she heard Eddie laughing with her father, who worked as a tailor from a shed in the garden.

She was still at the window when Eddie entered her room.

He had not knocked; he never did. Eddie was stocky and smooth-shaven and had thick eyebrows and wore a permanent smirk on his face.

'How's my little sister?' Eddie said. He closed the door behind him.

Mona did not reply but rose from her seat by the window, hitched up her skirt and went to lie on the bed. While she lay there, passive and inert, Eddie unbuckled his belt and climbed on top of her. Beneath Eddie's weight, his hot breath on her neck, she thought about Vincent and the happiness on the island where rivers rushed over white boulders on the journey to the sea. She imagined Granny Celeste shelling peas on the red porch, heard the nocturnal orchestras of the cicadas. Gradually these images and sounds faded and were replaced by a sluggish river laden with brown mud, broken branches and the bloated carcasses of dead animals and the air was filled with the odour of putrid flesh. She writhed and twisted beneath Eddie whose pumping action became frenzied. Then he gasped and held her tight.

Eddie stood up, pulled up his jeans and buckled his belt. Beads of perspiration shone on his forehead. He spoke fast and nervously: 'My little sister is fine, eh? She'll keep our secret, won't she?'

His visit had lasted no more than ten minutes. When Eddie left Mona he threw under the bed the five-pound note he and two other brothers had been giving her since her schooldays. She went back to the window and noticed that there had been a slight drizzle outside, though there were only a few clouds in the sky and they were as white as snowflakes.

A little after midday Mona heard her father call her. She left her room and went downstairs. He met her at the bottom of the stairs and she followed him to his workshop. She rarely entered her father's workshop and always found the light there too bright.

Burt Xavier looked at his daughter with solemn tenderness and shook his head.

'You can't spend all your life in that room, you know,

Mona. There's a big world out there with plenty nice things. Clothes and boys.'

Mona's silence was inviolable.

Burt sighed exasperatedly and said: 'Ah just finish this suit for Mr Singh, you know, the Jamaican coolie. Take this to his yard for me.'

Mona liked her father. She had often overheard him defending her against her mother, who treated Mona with punctilious care, but it was a punctiliousness devoid of any genuine affection. She, Antoinette Xavier, was a busy woman. Her five sons – Mona was her last child and only girl – had exhausted her supply of maternal care. She was forever visiting them, meddling in their marital affairs, and in return they showered her with gifts. She had little time for Mona. Burt Xavier, on the other hand, working from home, saw more of Mona and took greater interest in her. He believed it was just a matter of time before Mona adjusted to life in London. He often reminded Antoinette that it had after all taken them over a decade to find their feet here and they had come as adults. He reminded her of the early days when the only place they went outside work was the Caribbean Sunset Café, for the occasional dance. 'We were scared. Just like Mona.'

He lifted a brown parcel from a table cluttered with scraps of cloth, measuring tapes and scissors. Gilbert Singh's address was written on it. But Burt Xavier spelt it out, pronouncing every word clearly as if he were speaking to a child.

'Ah would bring it meself, but Ah have another job to finish by this evening. Hurry now. Ah did promise to get it to him by this morning. And don't go wandering off, make sure you're back before dark or else you might meet the Dundus.' He smiled at his daughter and she smiled back, weakly, and, so it seemed, without understanding.

Mona put on her coat, and, with the parcel under her arm, left the house. She passed boys throwing coins against the walls, girls playing hopscotch, a long queue outside the shop on Chatsworth Road which sold Caribbean food. The screeching noise of a car braking too suddenly caused her to jump and she almost turned back out of fear. But Mona was above all an obedient young woman. She did whatever she was told.

Gilbert Singh was alone. He took the parcel from Mona at the door, thanked her and said: 'Come in, nuh? Come in.'

From somewhere in the distance, above the sound of the traffic outside and Gilbert Singh's furious heavy breathing in her ears, Mona heard Granny Celeste calling her. Granny Celeste was calling the way she used to call Mona from among her friends, in a light, reproachful, part-cheerful voice: 'Mona, my love, enough play for now. Come inside.'

She heaved Gilbert Singh aside, and he fell off the settee with a bumping sound. He stared at her incredulously as she adjusted her clothes. Then she walked towards the front door.

'Mona, you won't tell, will you?' Gilbert shouted after her. 'You won't tell, will you? If you do I'll say is you trouble me, that it was always you who troubled me.'

He was still shouting when she banged the door shut. As she walked away from Gilbert Singh's house, a ringing sound grew in her ears. The leaves on the trees and hedges seemed luminously bright, the sky seemed somehow lower, as if she could reach up and touch it, grab a piece of that glassy blue. The people she passed, women and children, either glowed with a brilliant aura of happiness or a weak pallid light of misery. It was mostly misery. She could both see and feel their suffering, as if she could step into people's consciousness and know the intimate details of their private longings, the untold untellable stories of how they had survived from birth. She saw death too, saw it in the eyes of the old men and women, saw it in the children even.

She crossed over Lower Clapton Road and headed towards Chatsworth Road. Here she was almost brought to her knees by the scents and emotions that emanated from the shoppers. With people swirling around her, she clung to a lamppost for support but nobody noticed her, except for a man who emerged from the passing stream of pedestrians to offer his help. But she saw in his eyes a lust so violent that it frightened her and she hastened away.

Her heart was racing and she was sweating as she came upon the Caribbean Sunset Café. She tried to enter because some vague thought told her she would be safe there: Boswell would protect her. But the door was locked. She hurried away, walked through concrete estates and crossed the bridge which brought her onto Hackney Marshes. Now as she walked along the canal and under a bridge she collapsed with exhaustion, shivering and sweating.

Suddenly Mona saw in front of her an elderly woman who looked familiar. She wore a billowing white dress and her hair was tied in a checked red and white cloth. The woman reached out her hand and said: 'Come, my child.' When she spoke Mona saw that it was Granny Celeste. 'Come, my child. You are not for this world.' She took Granny Celeste's hand and instantly she felt relief from all the suffering she had endured.

Granny Celeste led her to the edge of the water, the brackish green water of the canal, and said: 'You have no need of this body now. For you are not for this world.' Still holding Mona's hand, she pushed the superfluous body into the canal, and Mona felt herself floating up, up into the sky. But the air felt wet and cold and slimy, and she started to cry.

'Hush, little baby,' said Granny Celeste. 'It's warm where we're going. Ever so warm.'

Chapter Fifteen

The slimy dark green water of the River Lea – centuries ago a mile wide in parts, now no more than twenty yards – flowed sluggishly eastwards. It would continue its torpid journey through empty industrial estates, under rotting bridges, in underground channels until its polluted waters reached the grand old man of the city, the River Thames. But here on Hackney Marshes it looked like a stretch of water with no origin and no destination. Boswell took one last pull on his cigarette and flicked it into the river and watched the butt drift until it lodged into the spokes on the wheels of a motor-bike which protruded from the water like the rusting carcass of some ancient mechanical beast. On the other side of the river two stout men hobbled around a golf course. From behind him came the puffing, panting hoarse shouts and whistles of various football matches. He turned now to face west and that part of the marsh where men in strips of blue and white, red and white, ran about excitedly as if enacting an ancient ritual, while between the pitches a few spectators stood about clutching Thermos flasks. Beyond the players, beyond the wide flat marshes, the five white tower blocks of Clapton Park Estate looked down with indifference.

He walked away from the river and up the gentle slope of the path that circled the playing fields. His footsteps on the gravelled surface were now one of many sounds in a landscape which somehow managed to appear bleak and desolate, though surrounded by the city. When he reached the white shed, a concrete structure which seemed to serve no purpose other than as a landmark, he stopped and waited. He was due to meet Darius Benedict here as he had done for the past three weeks every Saturday at tea time.

The detective's surveillance of Lorette had so far yielded

nothing. Boswell had read, with a mixture of relief and frustration, Darius Benedict's copious notes on her daily movements. The only thing he had learnt was that Lorette was a creature of habit. Her day would begin around 10 a.m., three hours after he'd left home, and for the rest of the morning she would read the newspapers. Early in the afternoon she would leave the flat to do her shopping. Twice a week she went to Ridley Road market in Dalston and on other days the supermarket in Stamford Hill. On returning home she would eat a light lunch while watching the news on television. Then around mid-afternoon she would run herself a hot bath, in which she would sit for forty-five minutes. After that she either took a siesta or played the piano for an hour. At no point over the three weeks had she received visitors or visited a soul. Her shopping expeditions, undertaken with ritual slowness, were never interrupted by conversations with friends.

To obtain this detailed picture of Lorette's daily routine, Darius Benedict had watched the house every hour of Boswell's absence. Twice he had impersonated council officials, once a pest inspector and another time a maintenance engineer. He had followed her through the market, and supermarket, observed her movements around the house through a telescope and even planted a listening device in the bedroom.

Whatever security Boswell derived from these weekly reports, however, was being undermined by a new and rapidly growing suspicion which was causing him no end of unease. Darius Benedict had delivered the first two reports with reassuringly professional detachment. Lorette had been referred to throughout as 'the subject' or 'Mrs Anderson'. But halfway through the third report – which was no different from the previous two in the routines recorded – that formal address was suddenly replaced by 'Lorette'. Intermittently, the writer used words like 'lovely' to describe a dress Lorette was wearing, she walked 'gracefully' in another sentence, and describing her having her hair pressed he observed that she looked 'sad'. Boswell was sure that Darius Benedict had fallen in love with Lorette.

He disliked Benedict even more than when they first met.

Something about the man's irrepressible optimism offended Boswell's own somewhat sepulchral disposition. There was too Darius Benedict's distasteful line of work. Benedict claimed that it was the reports of the Dundus which had inspired him to start his detective agency. If so, he had found his true vocation. He seemed to derive a sick pleasure from his job, trawling through the effluvia of marriages poisoned by mistrust and betrayal.

Seeing Darius Benedict making his way across the marsh agitated Boswell. He was anxious for this last meeting to happen and end; then he would be rid of this man who knew everything – or almost everything – about his life. Darius Benedict would become part of a memory of a temporary phase of madness caused by the strength of Boswell's love for Lorette.

'Ah, Mr Anderson,' Darius Benedict said as he approached. 'Sorry I'm so late. I was on schedule until I reached the canal. Quite a commotion over there. Poor girl. I was passing by just as they were hauling her body out of the water.'

'What are you talking about?'

'A girl drown,' Darius Benedict pointed in the direction of the tower blocks. 'Black girl, too. Shame, real shame. She look so young and innocent.'

Boswell had heard the ambulance sirens but in a neighbourhood where night and day were frequently punctuated by sirens he had not taken any notice. Now he was too preoccupied with his own affairs to give the matter any consideration.

Darius Benedict handed Boswell the final report. Boswell opened it and scanned the first page, which read like the first page of the first report.

'Nothing. If your wife's having an affair, Mr Anderson, I'm the reincarnation of Shaka Zulu.'

Boswell frowned: 'Well, I guess it was just my imagination.'

'Happens like that sometimes. Least you know now. No more sleepless nights, no more worries. She's safe.'

Boswell handed the private detective some crisp twenty-pound notes, the final payment for his services. Money which he had hoped to use in the poker game. He watched the detective count the notes, flicking them to ensure that two weren't stuck together.

Boswell wanted to bring this meeting to a speedy close. 'Thanks,' he said, and started to walk away.

'Er, there's just one more thing, Mr Anderson,' Darius Benedict said.

'What?'

The two men stood facing each other. In the distance a referee's whistle pierced the air like the cry of a wounded bird. A few spectators clapped and shouted excitedly, and the wind rushed through a cluster of trees.

'I've tried to report only the facts. Only things I've seen and heard. You paid me to watch your wife and report on her movements, I did just that. From what I saw and heard Lorette, er, your wife, is faithful. But, you know, I can't help feeling that something strange is going on with her. Something not right.'

'Sounds to me like you're trying to hustle some more work, like you want another month on the case.'

'No. No, I wasn't saying that.'

'Good. 'Cause you clean me right out.'

'Look, it isn't my business any more, Mr Anderson, so I don't have to say this. Everything I wrote in those reports is true. But I can't blame you for being suspicious. Your wife's behaviour is a little odd, especially in the afternoons. I can't understand why she draws the curtains.'

'Hmm, yes, I noticed that, too. I guess it's just a habit from back home. Protect the furniture from the strong sunlight.'

'In England, Mr Anderson?' Darius Benedict said sceptically. 'But as I said, didn't ever see anybody come or go. But the times I interrupted her, she looked so uneasy, as if, as if . . .'

'As if what?' Boswell demanded.

'As if by calling I had chased somebody away; you know, sort of flushed, like she just finished making love.'

'Why the hell didn't you say this before?' Boswell demanded. He stepped closer to Darius Benedict, angry, his fists clenched.

''Cause I reported what I saw and heard. I'm now telling you what I felt. But I ain't got no proof for that.'

'Damn, damn,' Boswell said. He turned and marched away. He walked at a furious pace until he reached the bridge over the canal which leads to Clapton Park Estate. Some of the spectators who had witnessed the removal of Mona's body from the canal milled about talking. Boswell ignored them. His mind was in turmoil. The certainty, the peace of mind Benedict had promised, and for which he had paid, was eluding him. Benedict had actually worsened matters, his reports now seemed meaningless, fraudulent; and his motive for sharing his intuitive reading of the case deeply suspect. Damn fool, damn idiot, Boswell cursed. These curses were directed at Benedict as well as himself.

On the other side of the bridge, he decided, with fearful reluctance, that he would have to confront Lorette. He rehearsed what he would say: 'Are you having an affair, Lorette?' No, he decided. That's too tentative, uncertain. He would accuse her. 'Lorette, I know you're having an affair.' He heard Lorette's response: 'What proof do you have?' He would reply, 'Because I can smell the interloper's scent when I get home.' He heard her laugh and this imagined laughter echoed with ridicule and contempt. No, he would have to give it very careful thought.

The Lord Nelson pub seemed the best place to sit and plan his next and final step for ending this hateful situation. But within minutes of entering the pub, he was given the news of Mona's death. He listened with disbelief to some hazy details from two drinkers and then set off for Burt Xavier's house.

Chapter Sixteen

Blake was going through a rough time, rougher than usual. Since Sheila's departure he had developed the habit of parking his car opposite the house he had burgled in Highgate. He would drive there late at night and sit in his souped-up Mini Clubman. When the occupants of the house – he only ever saw their silhouettes against the curtains – had retired for the night, he would wait a while, then drive away. He wanted to see her, the seductress, just one more time, and this desire had become an obsession. Afterwards he would drive slowly down to King's Cross, and play the fruit machines in the amusement arcades, drink a beer on the street corner and talk to some of the dope dealers and pimps who hung about there. He would arrive home just before daybreak and sleep till early afternoon. On waking up he would sit at the window of his fourteenth-floor flat and look down over the marsh, over its bleak beauty, its changing light as the day closed. Sitting there watching the marsh, he would be aware that his behaviour had become odd, and he feared for his future, but felt unable to do anything about it.

One day, Blake imagined that he saw the woman from the Highgate house wandering across the open space below. She stopped and beckoned to him. He grabbed his coat and dashed down the fourteen flights and onto the marsh. But when he got there he saw only schoolchildren. He wandered around in a state of agitation, urging himself to some sense of normality. When he had calmed down he decided to visit his mother.

Carmen lived in a tiny Samuel Lewis Trust Dwellings flat on Dalston Lane. The flat's proximity to Ridley Road market compensated for its pokiness and the faint but omnipresent odour of fried fish that clung to its walls.

Walking through the courtyard of the Samuel Lewis Trust building, he stopped briefly to watch a fight between two boys. They were both black, one was darker than the other, and both about the same size. Goaded on by their friends, the two boys rolled on the asphalt in a flurry of fists and feet. A spectator threw a length of wood at the combatants. The two boys scrambled for it and the boy with the lighter complexion reached it first. Now armed he rained merciless blows on his opponent, shouting, 'I'm going to kill you, nigger, I'm going to kill you, coon, wog.' An older boy broke up the fight and the crowd dispersed laughing.

Blake made a mental note to remember the boy who had won. He knew a gangleader who was constantly on the lookout for new recruits with the right temperament.

He found his mother, Carmen, with a visitor, a smooth-skinned golden-faced man who smoked Gauloises cigarettes and wore a white silk shirt and shiny grey suit. Blake radiated an intimidating proprietorial air. But it seemed to make no impression on the stranger. Still seated, Marvin, as he was called, stretched his long thin body and watched the horse-racing on the television.

Carmen went into the kitchen and Blake followed her, suppressing his annoyance at the stranger's presence.

'How you doing for money, Mummy?' he said.

'As usual. A million bills to pay,' she said, but not sounding in the least like a person burdened by unaffordable bills. Her voice had a lightness, a vague note of felicity, which made her sound young.

Blake had reached into his pocket for some money when sonorous laughter erupted in the living room.

'What's tickling you, Marvin?' she shouted.

'Your boy,' Marvin called back. 'Carmen, how can you let a big man like that still call you Mummy?'

Seized by anger, Blake rushed into the living room. Carmen reached out to stop him but she only snatched at the air. Blake, smouldering with fury, hovered over Marvin. 'It's none of your frigging business what I call my mother,' he said.

Marvin did not stir. With large, rather beautiful eyes, he

calmly looked up at Blake as if daring him to strike the first blow, as if warning him that it would be his last. It was the cold, imperturbable gaze of a man who had killed.

Carmen defused this potentially violent confrontation. From behind she held Blake's shoulder in a tender but firm grip and cooed: 'Come away, Blake. Don't mind Marvin. He's always laughing at people.'

'Well, it ain't right, a big man like him calling you Mummy. It ain't –'

'Shut up, Marvin,' Carmen said sternly, turning a passive Blake round. 'Anyway, I thought you were going to the bookies. Go on. Put a bet on for me, too, and I'll see you in the Lord Nelson later.'

Marvin departed at a leisurely pace. Blake was consoled by a feeling of triumph, which evoked memories of an earlier age when he and Barry would throw temper tantrums that compelled Carmen to choose between her sons and her current lover.

Carmen brought in some tea and biscuits, which Blake leapt on eagerly. He did not notice the solemnity with which Carmen attended to him, the wistful look in her eyes.

Seeing her go to the balcony to look out, Blake said: 'You're not looking for that Marvin bloke, are you, Mummy?' He sniggered.

'No, no,' Carmen replied abstractedly. 'I was thinking about Barry. He seems to get worse every time we visit.'

'Barry will be alright, Mummy. Give him time.'

'Maybe if I could get away from this estate into a house with a garden Barry could come and live with me when he's a little better.'

'A house, where?'

'I don't know, Blake. Anywhere else outside this miserable estate, beyond Dalston Junction. I feel like I have failed you boys. And God knows, I tried not to.'

'You haven't, Mummy. It's not your fault that Barry lost his marbles. It had nothing to do with you.'

A moment of silence passed between them.

Then Carmen said: 'I used to dream, you know. Used to

dream about a nice big house with a big garden and growing roses, and wearing fine clothes. I don't any more. I don't dream any more.'

'Come on, Mummy, you've got nice clothes. What about that dress I gave you for your last birthday? Cost me a fortune. You look great in it. And just wait until I hit the big time. You and Barry and me, we'll live in the biggest house in Hackney.'

A tear escaped and Carmen wiped it away before facing Blake. 'Blake,' she said cautiously, 'I think Marvin's right. You should stop calling me Mummy. You're too old for that.'

'Who's bloody Marvin to say what I should call you?' he exploded. He pushed away the tea and biscuits in anger.

'Please, Blake, calm down. I'm in love with Marvin. He wants to marry me.'

'He what? That, that . . .' Blake was stunned, nonplussed.

'Yes. He wants to marry me,' Carmen said, holding her chest. 'He loves me and I'm over forty years old and I need a man, Blake. I need company. I need somebody who can make me feel alive other than when I'm in the Lord Nelson drinking or at Dougie's dancing. I need somebody to wake up next to. I need somebody to love. If I let Marvin go I might never get another chance . . .'

Blake stared at his mother with incredulity and sudden hatred. He had seen many men pass through her life, but none had stayed for long. Now, less than a year after Barry had gone into hospital, she was proposing to marry. In his enraged eyes she had not only given up on Barry, she was denying him the only chance he ever had of winning the affection she had lavished on Barry. She was signalling in crystal-clear terms her lack of faith in him.

'What about Barry?' he said.

'I don't know, Blake. I pray for the day he gets better. But I don't know. Marvin . . . knows about him . . .'

Suddenly Blake could not contain himself any longer. He spat at his mother the meanest imprecations that came to mind: 'Slut, whore, bitch, old cunt . . .'

'Please, Blake,' Carmen said pleadingly. 'You've got your

whole life ahead of you. Don't ruin my one chance for happiness.'

Blake did not hear Carmen's entreaty, only the echoes of his angry and frustrated words. They were not the words he wanted to use; the very opposite. Filled with remorse and rage he walked to the window and punched the glass, and the noise of breaking glass resounded through the estate. Blood dripping from his wrist, he turned and glared at Carmen like a hurt child. Finally he pulled out a wad of notes, loosened some and threw them at her. 'For your wedding,' he said in a tone of chilling bitterness. Then he walked out, leaving a trail of blood, slamming the door behind him.

At the bottom of the stairs, Blake heard Carmen calling down the stairwell, 'Please, Blake, please forgive me.'

He paused momentarily then dived into the light of the afternoon.

Chapter Seventeen

On a wet, windy Wednesday, nine black Daimlers, grim and stately vehicles, squeezed through a narrow Homerton street lined with plane trees and came to a silent halt outside the Xaviers' house, a terraced cottage that Mona Xavier had known as an unhappy home in her short life. The first car carried the oak coffin in which Mona Xavier would be buried. The others, Mona's parents, her five siblings and their wives and children, and numerous distant relatives.

By the time the Xavier clan had covered the nine black Daimlers in wreaths, and filled the leather-bound interiors of those grim and stately vehicles, more cars, though less auspicious, had arrived. And they continued arriving, battered old Fords and Rovers, sitting low on the road. Some brought passengers drawn here by the various apocryphal tales that had been circulating since her death: of the black girl who had drowned herself in the canal and whose drifting corpse left a trail of tiger lilies on the canal's surface; of the description of her spirit floating up to the clouds, told by a gentleman who lived on the sixteenth floor of one of the tower blocks beside the canal; of Mona Xavier who had been pregnant and committed suicide because of unrequited love; of Mona Xavier who had been killed by the unsightly figure that was stalking the neighbourhood. Irresistibly drawn by these various tales of suicide and sanctification, it seemed the whole of Hackney was attending the funeral of Mona Xavier. They continued arriving even as the funeral procession moved off, led by the Daimlers driven by expressionless whitemen in black suits. It entered Homerton High Street and passed Hackney Hospital, where Mona had worked briefly in the canteen. And from behind the walls of that fortress of madness, the patients and inmates released an eerie sound: a chilling cry full of pain and mystery and longing. The procession proceeded past the library, the Anglican church, the fire station; the secondary school that Mona had attended. Here the pupils defied their teachers' orders and abandoned their desks to stare from open classroom windows to catch a glimpse of the funeral passing by below in silent solemnity.

Boswell, with Lorette, was in one of the last cars. Mona's death had sobered Boswell, made him aware that he was losing his grip. He had retrieved the amiable mask that his marital troubles had destroyed. He was drinking less and presented his normal smart appearance to the world. Such was his control, that he had not even batted an eyelid when Burt Xavier informed him that the funeral service for Mona would be held in the Church of Revelation and Redemption. What his fellow mourners would see, he had resolved, was the proprietor of the Caribbean Sunset Café and his wife, not their rocky marriage, not his hatred of the Reverend Mordecai Morris, into whose domain only his affection for the deceased was bringing him.

Boswell felt Lorette shift beside him. Her movements were stiff, as if, like himself, she were trying to hold something in. What a difference between now and the last time we went out, he thought. He had not watched her dress in preparation for this sad occasion. He had dressed in the spare room, where he now slept most nights, because, in the bedroom, the scent of betrayed love was now constant, even above the scent of the most piquant perfume. But neither had been able to break the silence of resentment and suspicion that clouded their lives.

The funeral service had begun by the time Boswell and Lorette reached the Church of Revelation and Redemption. This would be Boswell's first visit here in the ten years since he and the Reverend Mordecai Morris declared a truce. None the less, crossing the threshold of the Reverend Mordecai's domain induced in him a distinct feeling of unease: the hair on the back of his neck tingled and his stomach felt empty. But Boswell's discomfort wasn't evident; his face wore the same mournful mask as the other hundreds of people who had unexpectedly turned out to make Mona's funeral the largest that Hackney had seen in living memory.

Somebody said there were seats upstairs, and he and Lorette squeezed their way through the crowded lobby and climbed to the mezzanine which spanned the rear of the church. Here all the pews were full too, but two youngmen dressed in navy-blue suits, with identical haircuts which made them look like members of a tribe, gave up their seats to the proprietor of the Caribbean Sunset Café and his beautiful wife.

The high wooden altar was draped in wreaths and sorrow hung in the air like vines in a forest. The low sobbing of Antoinette Xavier, Mona's mother, was audible between the hymns and dedications. Now and again other female relatives of the deceased would add their plaintive voices to hers. During the singing of 'Onward Christian Soldiers', Boswell glanced at Lorette and noticed her dabbing her eyes.

The Reverend Mordecai Morris, who had opened the service with uncharacteristic restraint, now stepped forward, closer to the coffin. He took a deep breath, which inflated his already broad chest. He dramatically threw his head to the ceiling of varnished wooden rafters, then to the floor, plunging the entire church into a silence. Then in a voice so deep and sonorous, he called out: 'Lord, I am coming home, I am coming home, my Lord, Lord, I am coming home.' And he shook his head violently from side to side, and from within the congregation the echo of a woman's voice returned: 'Yes, my Lord, I am coming home.'

The Reverend Mordecai continued, now in a softer tone, though no less voluminous: 'Just turn twenty-one, Lord, and I'm coming home from this life, departing this body, this flesh joining you in the spirit, my Lord, where my soul can find peace, at the centre of your all-enfolding embrace, Lord, I am coming home. Just turn twenty-one, and I have seen enough sins, my Lord . . .'

'I am coming home, Lord,' shouted Sister Floella Simpson. She was near the front, beside a metal column, and like that column, without Sister Floella Simpson, the roof of the

Church of Revelation and Redemption would come tumbling down. Spirits regularly spoke through her. Her voice had a metallic quality, which had the extraordinary effect of bringing the Reverend Mordecai Morris's sermon to a halt: 'Yes, my Lord, coming home. I've known sin more than beyond my years, the wicked have cast their eyes on me, and though I walked amongst them doing no evil, the wicked, my Lord, lusted after my young body, used it and soiled it, and throughout my suffering, my Lord, I prayed to you for strength, for guidance, for love, yes, Lord, for a love I could not find since Granny Celeste departed, and oh, how I am happy, my Lord, to be reunited with the only source of mortal love that I knew. Thank you, my Lord, for calling me home. For the places I called home in that life that ended in the cold canal of the marshes, were not homes, but places of torment and humiliation and degradation, yes, Lord, in the very bed where I laid my head to rest each night, in the place of my labour, Lord, thank you for sending the Dundus to punish the wicked. Thank you, Lord.'

Sister Floella Simpson was now shaking like a fig tree in the wind. Beads of sweat glistened on her forehead. Unsteady on her feet, she lurched forwards, then backwards. Fortunately Sister Baker caught her by the shoulders and Sister Floella Simpson threw her head back and hollered: 'Yes, Lord, I am coming home.' And with that she expired in her sister's arms.

Boswell doubted that the revelation had been heard or understood by everybody in the church, as most people were distracted by the dramatics of Sister Floella Simpson's brief possession. But, looking down on the main body of the church, he noticed the distress on the faces of some of Mona's brothers. He did not expect, however, the accusing and condemnatory glances that some of the elderly women threw at him. He could almost hear them whispering: 'I knew no good would come out of that poor girlchile working with that Bosy Anderson.'

These were the women who knew the Caribbean Sunset Café in its earliest days, when it was a place of ill repute in the neighbourhood. They had not heard that Boswell Anderson had become a reformed character. Perhaps even if they did, none would have believed it.

'Come home, my Lord,' the Reverend Mordecai Morris – who had been muttering, 'I'm coming home,' like a man in a trance – bellowed once more. 'Coming home, my Lord,' and the choir started up, singing softly 'I Once was Blind'.

Boswell now recalled that afternoon when he had to comfort a distraught Mona, and now realised why she was in such a state. He watched the brothers hang their heads in shame and wiped his forehead, perplexed that he should have been implicated in Mona's farewell revelation.

With the singing of 'Amazing Grace', calm was restored in the church. The Reverend Mordecai Morris started reading Psalm 51: '"Have mercy upon me, O God, according to your lovingkindness: according to the multitude of your tender mercies blot out my transgressions. Wash me thoroughly from my iniquity, and cleanse me from my sin."'

Lorette cleared her throat and bowed her head. Boswell's eyes swept across the church, at the families gathered below and around him, the mothers holding babies, the children listening reverently, the family men he had known as boys, and he was filled with sadness. For he suddenly realised that he had never really won the fight with the Reverend Mordecai Morris. In fact, he had been defeated before the fight started. Here, at Mona Xavier's funeral service, he began to understand fully the nature and depth of his defeat.

The Reverend had tried to close down the Caribbean Sunset Café, rid the neighbourhood of that notorious habitat of pimps, gamblers, prostitutes. When Boswell saw his clientele disappearing, he went on the offensive with the help of young Belle Thompson. She was a streetwalker who possessed the remarkable and enviable talent of being able to pass for a girl ten years younger than her twenty-odd years. Following Boswell's instructions, Belle presented herself to the preacher as a homeless, parentless child. Mordecai Morris responded to her distressed presence as any man of the cloth would. He found her somewhere to live, invited her to join his flock and visited her regularly to comfort her with readings from the bible. But one night . . . It only happened once, but that one occasion was enough. Belle then claimed that she was pregnant and vanished, after receiving a handsome reward from Boswell.

When the embattled café owner confronted the preacher and threatened to expose him, the campaign to close the Caribbean Sunset Café was abandoned. Business had never recovered, but Boswell had maintained his side of the treaty and kept mum about the Reverend's dalliance with an underage prostitute.

Yet Boswell had never been happy with the strategy he had deployed to secure a truce. He had justified it to himself on the grounds that his back was against the wall, his livelihood threatened. But, like his accident-prone love life, it remained a troubling episode.

It seemed to him now, as he looked around the packed church, that he had never really understood what was at stake in that fight, not until this moment. While he had been offering nostalgia for the lush islands his customers and he had left, stirring it into the meals he served, dancing to it in the blues dances, stoking it up in his conversations, the Reverend Mordecai Morris had been dispensing something far, far stronger: faith. Faith in the present and the future, however wretched life seemed in England in those early years. He, Boswell, had been backing a losing horse. Faith had won over nostalgia. And his sadness deepened with the knowledge that it had taken the death of an innocent, simple child for him to recognise that defeat.

The funeral service passed without any further preternatural interruptions. But the effects of Sister Floella Simpson's revelation were visible as the mourners filed out of the church. Three of Mona's brothers, and an uncle who had rented a room in the Xaviers' house for some years, beat a hasty retreat. Antoinette Xavier, Mona's mother, supported by Burt and her sister, was led outside sobbing: 'I didn't know, I didn't know what was going on in my own house, with my own children. Oh God, forgive me. Mona, forgive me.' On the steps of the church, her knees buckled and four women rushed to her assistance, pushing Burt Xavier aside. He stumbled through the crowd, his head hung low in sorrow and dejection and guilt.

Boswell had noticed Gilbert's absence from the funeral service but had not dwelt on it. Now emerging from the church, he saw Gilbert standing on the other side of the street. The stream of mourners filing out caused Boswell to lose sight of him for a moment. He next saw him hastening away from the church. Watching Gilbert's flight, unusual because an occasion like this would be followed by drinking late into the night and shared reflections on the mysteries of life, Boswell was puzzled. Gilbert had not been to the Caribbean Sunset Café for days, nor had he visited the Xaviers to express his condolences. Boswell had last seen him, or rather his back, as he disappeared into the crowd at Ridley Road market. Why has Gilbert suddenly gone underground? he wondered.

Nearby a group of men had gathered around a latecomer who had brought a copy of the *Evening Standard*. Boswell caught a glimpse of the headline: 'Fear Stalks London's Inner City: Police Start Hunt for Mysterious Figure.' Those who had attended the service spoke excitedly of Sister Floella Simpson's allusion to the Dundus.

Boswell frowned and thought bitterly: Typical, we only make the papers when we do something scary.

Lorette, who was standing beside him, said: 'That was a lovely service, wasn't it, Bosy?'

He looked at her and said: 'Only if you have sins to atone for, and don't think that child ever harmed a soul.' He sounded tetchy, but the brief exchange seemed to break the ice that had set over their marriage in recent months. She put an arm through his and they set off home.

Chapter Eighteen

Segun Adebayo heard strains of classical music. The music thrashed his ears like the wind, and above it he heard a high-pitched noise like the motor of a machine. His leaden eyelids refused to open until he made a mighty effort. Light flooded his vision. Gradually objects began to take shape, solidifying from shimmering outlines, acquiring depth and colour: a pale pine writing bureau, a large Edwardian mahogany wardrobe, a low dressing table with an oval mirror, blue carpet and midnight-black micro-blinds. He tried to shift position and felt a sharp flush of pain in his back. He groped under the sheet for his body, which felt constricted and only vaguely attached to him. He lifted the sheet and saw that his torso was encased in brilliant white bandages, as if somebody had tried to mummify him. The metallic whine abated and the music followed soon. Fully conscious now, he remembered the chase, the fight, or rather the attack, and the cold, cold ground where he had felt such a terrible heat.

Suddenly the door opened and a woman with an olive complexion and dark brown hair came in carrying a vacuum cleaner.

'Oh, you're awake,' she said. Her voice was steady and soft.

'Where am I? Who are you . . . ?'

'Slow down, slow down,' she said. She placed the vacuum cleaner beside the Edwardian wardrobe. She approached the bed in silent steps, her movements graceful and light, almost feline.

'I'm Leah, and you're in my home, and you've been sleeping for almost two days.' Her voice was soft, almost a whisper. 'How do you feel?'

'Like I've been beaten up by the sea.'

She smiled as she hovered above him, and he saw now that her skin was taut and dry, which gave her smile a stiff reluctant quality.

'You must be hungry.'

He nodded, and she left the room, saying she would prepare him some food. Alone he felt somehow detached and disconnected from everything, as though he were not actually lying there, in that bed stiff and aching. Then fragments of more memories returned: a beach pummelled by giant waves and in the distance, on the horizon, ships; the smell of hot palm oil and roasted plantains, the taste of pepper; a low-ceilinged room, crowded and noisy. But friendship flowed in that room, and he wished now that he could be there, wherever it was, because with those memories came a flush of fear, as if the almost luxurious room in which he lay concealed a perilous secret, something terminal.

She returned to the room bearing a tray, placed it beside the bed and urged him to eat. This was unnecessary. At the sight and smell of the bowl of chicken soup and the plate of potatoes and spinach and a slice of steak, Segun raised himself upright and launched into the meal with ravenous gusto. By the time he had finished he felt stronger, but he still could not remember anything before or beyond the chase. Nor could he dispel or quieten the curious unease which his apparent saviour and hostess aroused. Sated, he lay back and drifted off to sleep.

When he woke again, she was sitting beside the bed. She had changed her clothes. She had been wearing a red kaftan before, now she wore jeans and a shapeless green pullover. Her hair was tied back, giving her a more youthful appearance.

'How are you feeling now?' she asked. Her pale green eyes bored into his with an intensity which further unsettled him.

'Much better, thanks. Have I been sleeping long?'

'No, only a few hours. You're on the mend. You're lucky; they could have killed you.'

'They?' He was puzzled.

'Whoever beat you up. Don't you remember?'

Now it came back to him more fully. He remembered that he had been driving a car when, for reasons which were still unclear, he gave chase to a group of boys. But events leading up to the chase were beyond his recollection. He could remember leaving Nigeria, but not why. There was a huge dark hole in the tapestry of his memory and the more he probed it the larger and emptier it seemed.

Leah told him that, unable to sleep that night, she had gone for a walk and was returning home when she came upon his prostrate body, the retreating footsteps of the men she assumed had been his assailants still audible. What was a single white woman doing walking around at an ungodly hour in a neighbourhood where any sensible law-abiding citizen owned a dog for the purpose of deterring burglars, or for protection during even the shortest night-time stroll? She said she periodically suffered from insomnia and long late-night walks helped her to sleep. For protection she always carried a plethora of self-defence gadgets – an aerosol can of ether, a battery-powered alarm. Besides, that night she had been looking for somebody. It seemed that a month ago, on one of her nocturnal strolls, a bizarre figure had tried to frighten her. It had leapt from behind a car some yards ahead of her, arms raised, its shaggy, gold-coloured cape glittering under the streetlight. She had stood her ground, and was reaching for her can of ether when she saw the eyes beneath the black mask and knew that she would not come to any harm.

'Weren't you scared?' Segun asked.

'No. Not at all. In fact, I sensed great pain from it, or him. I reached out towards him, but he turned and ran. I've not seen him since but several times a week I go looking for him. I sense he's somebody in need of help.'

'But you found me,' he said.

'Yes,' she said, smiling.

After struggling home with Segun – she lived only a few minutes' walk from where he was attacked – she had bandaged him up and had called in one of her colleagues, a doctor, from the hospital.

'Why are you being so kind?'

'Must be my Christian background,' she said, smiling sardonically.

'What about your husband? Doesn't he mind?'

'Oh, I am single. I live here alone; and even if I did have a husband it wouldn't have made any difference. You're in need of care, and I'm trained to care for people.' There was a casualness in her voice, as if she were regularly in the habit of bringing home injured strangers.

'Where are you from? My colleague, David, thinks you're South African. I think you're Nigerian.'

Segun had a sudden vision of them standing over him debating his country of origin. He recalled now a moment of semiconsciousness when he imagined he was lying on the forest floor surrounded by swaying trees with silver leaves which rustled in the wind.

'Nigeria,' he said.

'I was right, then.'

'How did you know?'

'Oh, I spent a year doing voluntary service in a hospital in Freetown in Sierra Leone, and one month me and some friends travelled to Accra and Lagos.'

'You been to my country. I'm from Lagos. Maybe we even passed each other on the street.'

'I doubt it. We were only there for a week. It was a disaster. My friend was in love with a Nigerian doctor. He had told her to come, he would marry her. But when she got there she discovered he already had six children and two wives. She's still in Africa, though. Last time I heard from her she was in Uganda working with Aids victims.'

'And you, didn't anybody propose to you in Africa?'

'More than I could cope with. But it's too hot there. I know everybody beats us at cricket and football and we've got a lousy government, but I decided after my year in Africa that I love this country.'

'I think I know how you feel. Lagos is dirty and smelly, but it's my home.'

'So what are you doing here?'

Her question struck him like a sudden roadblock on what had been until then a brightly lit, clear road. He searched for an answer, trawled his memory for some thought, but found nothing, only an impenetrably dark space.

She misunderstood his sudden silence: 'Sorry, I didn't mean it like that. I wondered whether you were a student or something.'

'No, don't apologise. It's just that I can't answer you. I don't know what I'm doing here, I don't know, I don't know.' There was dread and despair in his voice now, like the dread and despair of a man who had looked into a mirror and not recognised himself.

'No. Really, I'm sorry. You're tired and here I am badgering you with questions, preventing you from resting. I'll see you in the morning.'

She turned the light off on her way out. Leaving Segun staring into his opaque past, until a wave of exhaustion seized him and washed him onto the soft, secure shores of sleep.

When he next woke up, his head felt less fuzzy, and the pain had abated considerably. He called out for Leah, but no reply came. Seeing what he surmised were his clothes draped over a chair, he got up and dressed. He wandered along a corridor until he came to the kitchen. He had half expected to find Leah there, but it was empty. A note propped up against the radio read: 'Gone to hospital to stand in for sick friend. Back around 6 p.m. Please make yourself at home.'

Hunger gnawed at his stomach. So he prepared and ate a mountainous plate of scrambled eggs and toast and washed it down with two cups of black coffee.

He decided to explore the flat, this island onto which he had been washed up. He noticed a pet's feeding tray on the floor beside the refrigerator. A cat's probably. But he saw no other sign of an animal anywhere. From the kitchen, he wandered into a large airy room with polished floorboards and an immense floor-to-ceiling bay window. He assumed that this was the living room. Colourful framed prints hung on the walls. Walking around the room looking at these pictures, he was distracted by the sight of an empty birdcage.

He went to examine it and saw next to it, to his consternation, an aquarium with a dead goldfish lying at the bottom. Then he noticed the wilting fuchsia, its dried flowers strewn on the floor around it; and the dead yucca plant, its leaves brown and yellow. These signs of neglect notwithstanding, the room, as elsewhere in the flat, was generally tidy. And there was a cosiness about it which made him feel secure.

Back in the bedroom, he searched through his belongings – which Leah had placed on the table – for clues about himself. He found the talisman, and immediately recognised it as an object he deeply valued. He found, too, the distinctive green card with the legend 'AM Cars'. This opened another window into his past and he vaguely recalled that he had some connection with that card.

He telephoned the number and a familiar voice answered: 'AM Cars.'

'My name's Se-Segun, Segun Adebayo,' he stammered.

'Segun Adebayo,' the voice at the other end of the telephone repeated in recognition. 'Where have you been, man?' Before Segun could answer, the voice continued: 'It doesn't matter. Two men from immigration were here looking for you yesterday. They're out to deport you. Stay away for a couple of weeks. Keep low. We'll take care of them.' Then the speaker hung up the phone.

Segun slammed down the phone and staggered in bewilderment. Shards of memories of his life rained down on him: his last conversation with Victor, his fellow driver; watching immigration officials arrest another driver; the room where he lived with two other Nigerians. He emerged from this sudden storm understanding more about himself. Yet he felt that a vital piece of his life was still missing, an essential spark which would animate these disparate fragments, give them coherence and imbue them with purpose. If only I could remember, he thought frustratedly.

Leah returned a little after 6 p.m. Segun had been sitting in his room for several fruitless hours trying to find that final, essential clue to himself. He welcomed her presence as a diversion from the maddening stubbornness of his memory.

A few hours later they ate dinner, which Leah had cooked. She had changed from the nurse's uniform that she had been wearing on arrival. Segun had thought she looked compassionate, efficient and very attractive in it. Although the red frock she now wore did not have the same effect, he felt relaxed in her company. The apprehension he had felt earlier had been replaced by gratitude born of the recognition that he had been extremely lucky. She had probably saved his life. And he had begun to see in her home a refuge where he could recover, and hide.

Over dinner she told him she had read a newspaper report on the masked, costumed figure who had tried to frighten her. A St Lucian porter at the hospital had also seen it, and called it a Dundus. She said she had laughed at the man's suggestion that it was a supernatural being. Segun did not comment.

After dinner, they moved to the living room. Segun resisted passing any remarks on the dying plants, the vacant birdcage, and the fish tank with its dead goldfish. He was determined to be a model guest; polite, attentive, grateful.

Apart from enquiring about his day and health earlier that evening, Leah had shown no further curiosity about him. Her conversation over dinner had focused on her peculiar concern with the so-called Dundus, and herself. In the living room he heard more about her peripatetic childhood caused by her father's occupation as a soldier, about her birthplace in Wiltshire, about her rich genealogy – French, Persian, English, Indian somewhere – about her fondness for adventures in exotic lands, which never failed to increase her appreciation of her beloved England.

This eagerness to volunteer information about herself, which went beyond the conversational, roused in Segun a suspicion that his hostess was a deeply lonely person. Listening to her he recognised a loneliness which he himself had once known. How and when it had ended, though, was a mystery, part of that conundrum of his crucial missing piece of memory.

His mind had been drifting while Leah was recounting a

holiday she had had in Peru. He now turned his full attention to her again.

She was seated on the sofa, talking animatedly, unaware of his wavering concentration. Then she casually complained that her shoulders were aching, the result of helping to lift a nineteen-stone patient from his bed. She swivelled her arm and twisted her neck, and her face writhed in pain.

'Let me massage it for you,' Segun said.

'Would you? That's so kind.'

'It's the least I can do.'

She sat upright and he went over and began kneading her neck and shoulders.

'Ouch, ouch, that hurts.'

'Sorry.'

'Don't be. It's supposed to hurt. It shows that the muscles are bruised.'

Segun resumed, gentler this time. Leah fell quiet, but for occasional moans of relief as if Segun's fingers were ironing out knots and kinks in her muscles. After some minutes he said: 'Will you go in search of that thing, that man, the man in the golden cape and black mask, tonight?'

'No, I am too tired,' Leah said, sighing wearily, rolling her shoulders.

When his hands were tired he stopped but rested them on her shoulders. Reaching behind her, Leah clasped his left wrist and said: 'Segun, you can stay as long as you like. Stay with me.'

Segun's attentiveness had not matched his considerate gesture. His mind had begun to stray to that cul-de-sac in his memory which refused to yield its secret. But the pathos in her voice brought him back to the reality of the room, to the woman whose shoulders he had been kneading; this unusual woman who, searching the night for what sounded like someone or something, had saved his life and was now inviting him to share her life.

Involuntarily, he said: 'I don't think I have anywhere to go.' But even as he spoke, he glanced at the empty birdcage, and wondered what had happened to its occupant.

Chapter Nineteen

It was late afternoon and Boswell was alone in the Caribbean Sunset Café, which had not seen a single customer in days. Seated at the counter, he was trying to write a letter to Cleo. The evidence of his aborted attempts to compose an opening line was scattered at his feet. Writing, unlike talking, had never come easy to him, even at the best of times. Once committed to paper, words seemed to lose their ability to express how he felt, what he thought; made him doubt that he possessed any feelings or thoughts.

These were not the best of times either. Too much was happening around him; his concentration was weak. Earlier that day he had received an excited phone call from Stone Mason informing him that the poker game with T-Bone Sterling was on. He had forty-eight hours to get ready, and he'd spent most of his money employing Darius Benedict.

The advent of the poker game should have cheered him but it had not come at the most propitious time. Everywhere he went people were talking about the Dundus, speculating on whether it was a spirit or a human. The content of Cleo's letter hung over Boswell like a cloud of ill omen. Mona's suicide, and his friend Gilbert's as yet unknown role in her tragedy, troubled him like the aftershocks of an earthquake. Could he have prevented her death if he had been less preoccupied with his own affairs? Poor child, he thought. Poor, poor child. Maybe all she had needed was some kind person to hold her gently, once; just once, without desire, selflessly; some kind person to show her that this journey we call life is not all about sorrow, loss and tears.

A cold current coursed through him, and he shivered and wondered whether anybody would be there to hold him in his hour of need, which seemed imminent. He had not yet confronted Lorette about her mysterious behaviour; but he soon would, after the game. After the game. A mist of death and corruption and infidelity was obscuring his life when he most needed a clear head.

Boswell picked up his pen and made another effort to start the letter. He wrote: 'Dear Cleo, I have often wondered whether the gods who kill us for their sport, do us a far greater evil when they kill our dreams . . .'

He stopped there, because just then the café's door opened. He looked up and saw Carmen, whom he had not seen in two years. She walked directly to the counter, a half-smile playing on her lips. Her greeting sounded breezy, but resonated with the unburied feelings of shame and regret which had been colouring their rare encounters since she ended their affair.

'Hello, Carmen,' he replied casually, as if they had seen each other only yesterday. 'Weak milky tea, two sugars?' he added. In their years of intimacy he used to tease her about her fondness for that strange brew of warm, sweet watery milk laced with tea, which she, he believed, wrongly confused with what most people called tea. Her reaction, a smile of recognition of this old private joke, pleased him.

She took the nearest table to the counter. Boswell made two cups of tea, and joined her at the table.

'You're looking good,' Boswell said.

'Thanks. You're not looking too bad yourself.'

Boswell detected a strained effort on her part to appear more confident than she actually felt. How much courage she must have called up to visit him. Something had to be seriously amiss. Echoes of their last encounter reverberated in his memory: 'He's their father, Bosy, and yes, dammit yes, I still love him.'

Years ago she had wounded him, left him writhing in that inferno of the broken-hearted where, drunk and unwashed for days, he would prowl the streets at night, buying disposable love from ladies who plied their wares on railway sidings in Stamford Hill, or car parks in King's Cross. Hurried sex, fleeting comfort. Somehow he kept the Caribbean Sunset Café open. Solitarily sitting in its dark basement on Saturday nights waiting for the customers who had also drifted away, forever disappointed because times had changed and the blues dance was dying. Somehow he had crawled out of that pit of torment, told himself as he clung to its slippery side that her crime against his heart was no worse than that which he had experienced as a youngman. The girl who had betrayed him; the incubus of his exile.

'How's Barry? Blake hasn't mentioned him in a while. I'm sorry, eh.'

'He seemed much better when I last saw him. He's put on a lot of weight, though. They were about to start him on a diet and keep-fit routine.'

Her gaze wandered away from him as she spoke, drifted to the faded, stained green, yellow and black map of Jamaica with its portraits of the island's five national heroes. Her voice had lost its affected breeziness.

'Have they given you any idea when he might be able to come out?'

A hand roamed from the crow's-foot on her right eye, down her cheek to the laugh line at the corner of her lips, as if she were trying to erase these indelible signs of ageing. This gesture provoked in Boswell a surge of sympathy.

'No,' she replied. There was hopelessness in her voice. She continued: 'I'm not worried about Barry. It's Blake. I haven't seen him for two weeks. His phone just rings and rings. I've been to his flat three times now. Nobody's there. I don't know where he is.'

'Probably looking for you,' Boswell said.

Carmen looked at him quizzically. 'Blake doesn't have to look for me, Bosy. He knows very well where I live.'

'Does he? I saw him last week. He spent a few hours here. He looked as miserable as kid lost in a fairground.'

Boswell recalled to himself that Blake had turned up one late morning. He had sat where Carmen was now seated for a whole hour, sullen, pensive, silent. Boswell had been busy doing his end-of-month accounts and thought nothing of Blake's silence. When they eventually got to talking Blake revealed that he and Sheila had split up. But Boswell knew Blake well enough to know that Sheila's departure, for whatever reason, would not have such a visibly devastating effect on Blake.

As Blake was leaving the Caribbean Sunset Café, he said to Boswell: 'Did you know that my mom's gonna marry some guy called Marvin?' He did not wait for a response but departed immediately, leaving behind a puzzled Boswell to meditate on the bitter tone of the statement. He had not seen Blake since.

'Told me that you're planning on marrying. Congratulations.'

'Oh, that's still cutting him up, is it? There's nothing definite. I just mentioned it to him as something that might happen, that's all. I don't understand why he's so upset. Does he expect me to spend the rest of my life alone, playing mother to him? Now that Barry's —'

'I don't know what he expects, Carmen. Maybe he's missing Barry, maybe he does expect you to play mother to him now that Barry's not there. Isn't that what you were going to say: "Now that Barry's not there"?'

'Please, Bosy, don't bring up that old chestnut. I didn't mean it like that. Besides, Blake's not a child any more.'

A change in the timbre of Carmen's voice warned Boswell that they were straying into dangerous territory. An emotional jungle in which she had often mauled him for daring to intrude, forgetting that she had invited him there in the first place. Carmen's peculiar relationship with her sons. He threw a full stop at whatever remark he'd been about to make. And together they sat, these two ex-lovers, groping in their shared silence for some middle ground between love and hate.

Boswell had first met Carmen in the company of The Bird, the fabulous dancer and fickle father of her children. In the heyday of the Caribbean Sunset Café they were a special attraction of those sweaty Friday and Saturday night basement sessions. Their presence, his dancing, her beauty, enhanced the atmosphere. When The Bird danced, a circle of spectators would form around him, mesmerised by his shuffling feet, urging him on to rise, to float, to soar. Sweating and twirling a white handkerchief, he would laugh as he danced around the circle, towards and away from Carmen. As a prelude to his flight, he would plant a kiss on her flame-red lips, like a hummingbird feeding on a hibiscus; sidle away; then rise those almost imperceptible inches off the floor, all the while laughing. Boswell would watch enthralled like everybody else, grateful that this beautiful couple had chosen to grace his modest establishment.

He could not say when he started to desire her. But he knew with unshakeable certainty that The Bird would one day fly away because the man had that kind of look in his eyes: the look of mountains and seas, of warmer climes, of islands.

When Carmen started coming to the Caribbean Sunset Café alone amid rumours of The Bird's flight, Boswell bided his time. He watched patiently as she rejected a host of zealous but inept admirers; then signalled his own quiet desire by sending her a single red hibiscus. The next Saturday night, with Sunday morning bleeding through the clouds above the city, they danced a dance of lost love in the blues dance. Their bodies welded in the heat, her tears mingled with his sweat.

A month later, having consummated their love in Boswell's flat one afternoon, she invited him to meet her boys. An invitation that Boswell, who was unaware that she was a mother, accepted with disguised cool. He was surprised to meet two bright ten-year-old boys, full of energy and mischief and insatiable curiosity. Two fatherless boys who leapt on him with a hunger for rough play that exhausted and ener-gised him.

'For some reason, I don't know what, I feel that you're not going to run away,' she told him one night, as they lay in bed, the boys sleeping soundly from the drug with which she had laced their bedtime cocoa. (This was the only way to get Barry to sleep through the night.) Boswell was shocked by her insight and from that moment ceased to regard her as merely another conquest, as he had done with every woman he had slept with since Cleo.

'You mean, you knew The Bird would fly one day?'

'Yes, I knew all along. But he made me happy while he stayed.'

'And what if he comes back tomorrow?'

'This time I think he's gone for good.'

'You haven't answered my question.'

There was a long silence before she said: 'I don't know, Bosy.' Then in that darkened room, on that love-soaked bed, she rolled closer to him and held his naked damp body in an embrace which he would realise years later was a plea for forgiveness, for understanding, for selfless love. He returned her embrace, resigned, accepting the probability that he was keeping The Bird's bed warm until he returned.

So Boswell became a surrogate lover and a surrogate father, the latter role a consequence of the former. He could not have Carmen without her boys. Two years into this strange relationship, Boswell attempted to pull away, like a man suddenly aware of an unhealthy and growing addiction. Carmen begged him to stay, if not for her sake, for the boys'. Barry was fast becoming uncontrollable; and the borough council's social services department had more than once threatened to remove him from her care and place him in a home for difficult children. Boswell relented. After all, he liked the boys, especially Blake, who treated him like a father. Barry was difficult to like because he was constantly competing for Carmen's affection and attention. He daily threw temper tantrums or played mischievous pranks which, as he entered his teens, became progressively delinquent. Oh, how Boswell tried with Barry, enduring his offences, his belligerence, his sullenness. Oh, how he advised and coaxed and encouraged. But immured in their lives, enjoying a curious happiness from this domestic friction, he made the fatal mistake of forgetting that he was only a stand-in.

The Bird's return devastated him.

The Bird appeared one day at the Caribbean Sunset Café in a white linen suit and Panama hat, leaning with dandified insouciance on a gold-capped lignum vitae walking stick. A bit thicker around the waist, but no less nimble on his feet.

Full of fantastic tales about dancing on the streets of Port of Spain and Rio de Janeiro and New Orleans; unencumbered by remorse or guilt; expecting to resume where he had left off.

Boswell retreated, of course, satisfying himself with occasional visits from Blake who continued to seek his advice and sometimes brought messages of apology from Carmen. Two years later, the boys now sixteen, The Bird vanished again. And though Boswell knew that he could once again share Carmen's bed, that he could alleviate her – as well as his – pain, his pride conquered his heart.

That was five years ago, and many rivers had flowed under the bridge since. Now she sat before him in the Caribbean Sunset Café, one son incarcerated in a mental hospital, another driven to distraction by her neglect; flushed with hope for enduring love.

'What if The Bird comes back?' Boswell said.

Without hesitation, as if she expected this question, she said: 'Marvin loves me.'

Boswell looked into her eyes, looked deep and long and resisted observing to her that she had not answered his question. Again. But when he had considered her answer a little more he thought he understood her. She believed that Marvin would protect her against The Bird, should he return, protect her against her taking him back as she had done twice before.

'And I didn't,' Boswell said.

'You did in your own way, Bosy,' she said. She reached across the table and held his hand. 'But you didn't love me enough to save me from myself.'

'Did you expect me to fight The Bird for you?'

'No, Boswell, no, but . . .'

'Could I have won?'

She removed her hand, and his empty palm felt damp and warm. She shifted her gaze from him. He took her silence as an answer. After what seemed like an eternity of silence, she said: 'Are you happy, Bosy? Now that you're married? I'm really jealous of you. You must be happy.'

He laughed lightly, leaned forward and ran the index finger

of his right hand down her left cheek: 'You're such a child, Carmen. Such a child. There were times back then when I felt that I was being a father not just to the boys but to you as well.' They both laughed now.

Suddenly the door of the Caribbean Sunset Café swung open, and Gilbert entered timidly. He was a harrowing sight. White bristles covered his cheeks, his eyes seemed more sunken, and the darkness around them darker than usual. He was wearing a soiled white mac, which seemed far too large for him. He came straight to the table.

'B-B-Bosy, I m-m-must t-talk to you,' he stammered.

'Gosh, it's probably way after four and I have to get somewhere,' Carmen said, suddenly flustered.

Boswell told Gilbert to wait, and walked with Carmen to the door. As she hugged him and kissed his cheek, he said: 'Don't worry about Blake, he's not a kid. He's alright. I'll tell him you were looking for him when he comes by next time.'

'Thanks, Bosy.' She started to step through the door, then paused and said: 'You didn't answer my question. Are you?'

'What?'

'Happy.'

'That my oldest child might have finally found love? Yes.'

She shot him a puzzled glance, smiled and continued through the door.

'Good luck, Carmen. I really mean that.' He doubted that she had heard him above the traffic noise. But he knew that she knew, without having to hear it from him, that he wished her happiness. Whatever that is, he thought: that visitor had appeared to him in epiphanous moments, danced in the blues dance of his life, illuminating it now and again, but always melting back into the darkness.

'Lord, Gilbert, where you been all this time, man?' Boswell said at last to the dishevelled, haunted-looking figure whose gaunt face and neck protruded from the dirty, oversized mac.

'I'm going home, Bosy. I can't take it any more. I'm going home, man.'

Chapter Twenty

Segun Adebayo was sprinting along Upper Clapton Road, towards Stamford Hill. He ignored the pain in his legs, the burning sensation in his lungs. He was blind to the redbrick houses, the cars which screeched to a halt as he flew across junctions; deaf to their incensed, foul-mouthed drivers. He was running for his life, he was running for Sade.

For weeks he had wandered around Leah's apartment, struggling with that intractable part of his memory which he persisted in believing held some vital clue to the meaning of his existence. He had concealed his angst from Leah, who each day brought home some exquisite little present, a ring one day, a box of silk handkerchiefs with his initials, S.A. But he had continued to regard the empty birdcage and fishtank as ominous signs. The disturbingly swift demise of the flowers she bought daily – the lilies, chrysanthemums, roses and carnations that died in the night, as if some malevolent force had sucked them dry, leaving them brittle – had nullified the comfort of her gifts and heightened his distress.

Three days ago, or was it two? – each day had seemed to merge imperceptibly – she had thrown a party. She had paraded him before her friends as Segun Adebayo, her African friend, and her friends had launched into lengthy lamentations for the plight of his people and his continent, and the disappearing wildlife and plants. Some had talked about their roots and their antiquity. None had recognised his distress. None had seen his fear. He had felt invisible.

Then yesterday he had been out with Leah in Islington, trawling the antiques arcade for the perfect chaise longue. They had not found it. As they walked back to her car, parked on Islington Green, he had instinctively sensed familiar eyes watching him. He had glanced up at a passing 38 bus, and seen, framed by an upper deck window, a woman with eyes like all the hope in the world looking down on him. The bus had rushed by, swallowed by the road and the traffic, but a hologram of her face, visible only to his eyes, had hovered in the air, luminous and bright, like a full moon over the ocean. Her name had not come back to him immediately. But that fleeting sight of a face he had once known had stayed in his mind, agitated his sleep.

He had woken up that morning with his head clear of the fog of amnesia. The wall in his memory had been breached. The why? of his life had been revealed. Her name was Sade.

When Leah left for work at noon he had dressed in his old clothes and stolen away from the apartment, glancing back at the hallway where the lilies Leah had brought home the previous evening had already died.

Now, as he ran through Stamford Hill, skirting Hasidic Jews in their long dark coats, he was certain that he had escaped death. He was running for life and love.

At Seven Sisters station, Segun Adebayo boarded a Brixton-bound Victoria line train. The carriage was mostly empty, which he appreciated because he was somewhat dazed. The brightly lit interior rushing through the dark tunnel tossed him about as he struggled to regain his grip on reality. Did I live that experience or was it a dream? A bolt of pain stabbed his stomach, as if in answer to his question.

Suddenly the tunnel ended, the doors slid open and passengers boarded. Segun closed his eyes and hauled in his long legs so his bony knees jutted up. Folding his arms, he tried, without much success, to make himself seem tiny, insignificant, invisible.

The doors closed and the rustle of newspapers opening began as the train plunged again through the tunnel. A man in the seat opposite opened *The Times* and Segun saw the headline, 'The Inner City Beast' above a black-and-white photograph of a figure in a thick long cape and an elongated mask which merged into his chest. He could just make out the picture caption: 'Amateur Photographer David Smith's shot of the mysterious character who has been spreading fear throughout London.' The story accompanying the picture was unreadable from that distance. The train next stopped at King's Cross, the carriage filled up and the newspaper was lost from his sight. Segun was sandwiched between two burly men whose stomachs rose from below their chests like voluminous wind-filled sails. He tried to shrink even further, to become a momentary nothingness until he reached Brixton. At Oxford Circus, the carriage filled to beyond capacity and people stepped on his feet and knocked his knees with briefcases and handbags and umbrellas. From somewhere in the carriage, hidden from his view by the lower half of bodies which now seemed like tree trunks in a dense rainforest, came hissing music from a Walkman stereo. Between Green Park and Victoria the train crawled to a halt and remained motionless for several minutes.

When the seconds began passing slowly Segun Adebayo opened his eyes, and between the forest of legs he thought he saw a female passenger lower the magazine she was reading, lower it enough to reveal dark almond-shaped eyes which smiled at him invitingly. He closed his eyes and imagined that the now restless shifting and shuffling bodies were indeed plants in a forest.

He saw himself rise off the forest floor and everywhere was covered in a dark opacity. He stumbled forward and tripped over something, the roots of a tree, a ground vine. Then from the gloom came a babel of noise, as if nocturnal animals and plants were talking to each other. The noise grew in intensity and pierced his ear drum, causing him to clasp his ears in an effort to shut out the painful din. He fell to the damp ground and felt cold wet creatures slithering across his naked arms, neck and face. Terrified and weak he leapt up, stumbling forward. From nowhere a bird of fluorescent red shot through the darkness, like a spear ablaze.

The cacophony abated and he heard a liquescent melody like music from a band of marimba players, or a steel pan orchestra. It filled him with an unnatural thirst, induced visions of vast deserts of dunes undulating to the horizon, of sandstorms. Desperately, he pushed his pain-racked body in its direction. With each step, the air moistened and below the music he thought he could hear the susurration of grass and leaves. Then the music started climbing in volume, building up from a stream into a wide, turbulent river that tore its way through canyons and forests and plains, cascading down precipitous cliffs in a thunderous waterfall, the spray from which enshrouded the surrounding forest in a perpetual damp mist. The music stopped, leaving only a scraping noise, like the repeated abrasion of hard, dry grass over taut skin. Suddenly there was nothing except a harsh light followed swiftly by a rush of feet. He had reached Brixton and the end of the line.

All of a sudden he was awake and filled with purpose. He stepped into the stream of humanity flowing towards the escalator. At the top of the escalator he thrust his ticket to a collector, an African with a cherubic face and a toothbrush moustache; then he bounded up the stairs and stood in Brixton Road, a torrent of brown, black, white, pink, yellow, red faces and a deafening roar of traffic.

He turned towards the town hall, ignoring the higglers selling poster-prints, and cheap aftershave, the singers from the Brixton branch of the Church of Revelation and Redemption, the stocky, ragged black man, around whom the current of people flowed, leaving him in a circle as he delivered inaudible speeches. Segun passed the library, the town hall and was free from the crowd.

A mile further on he turned into a housing estate, and stopped to check a map of its layout. Identifying the building he wanted, he made his way there. It was a tower block, fourteen floors high with a hundred and forty flats. He did not have a number for Sade. So he decided to wait. It was almost the end of the working day and there was a steady flow of passers-by. He stopped everybody who passed and asked if they knew a Sade. The fearful, the indifferent hurried by, the curious passers-by stopped and after listening to his description of this Sade went on their way, their expressions varying from suspicious frowns to sympathetic but hopeless smiles. One middle-aged Jamaican lady teasingly told him that if he did not find his Sade he should come up and see her some time; she lived on the second floor. 'Ah not so young no more,' she said, her smile a cross between maternal goodness and feminine lewdness. 'Ah not so young no more, but Ah still talawa.' A nervous-looking youngman whose eyes were concealed by wraparound shades, and most of his face obscured by the huge collar of a large leather jacket asked Segun if he knew which flat he could get some E in. The youngman did not dawdle when Segun Adebayo looked at him with incredulity.

Finally an elderly gentleman, tall sprightly and skinny, came by. Segun approached him, saying: 'Good afternoon, sah, I'm looking for a Nigerian girl who lives with two other girls in this building. Her name's Sade.' He described her.

The old man's bloodshot eyes rolled, and he seemed to go into deep concentration. When he spoke Segun smelt rum, and thought immediately of Boswell Anderson.

'You know, there're some girls living next door to me. Africans. One of them could be her. From your description.'

Hope revived Segun's flagging morale. 'Where? Where?'

'Now hold on,' the old man said. 'Ah ain't saying is she. Ah saying it might be she. What you want she for, anyway?'

Segun began to tell his story. The old man interrupted him and said: 'Look, Ah ain't fit to stand and talk like this. Come upstairs, man, come upstairs.'

Segun followed him into the building up to the seventh floor. 'Shouldn't really be living this high up,' the old man said. 'Keep on complaining but they not listening to me.'

He lived in a one-bedroom flat with a view towards Clapham, a view over grey slate rooftops. On a steel-framed shelving unit was a large black-and-white gilt-framed portrait of a man who bore some resemblance to Segun's host. But while the old man had laughing eyes, the face in the portrait glared with a hypnotic severity, which held Segun's attention long enough for the old man to notice and remark: 'That's my father: a hard act to follow.'

Segun turned to his host.

'Name's the Mighty Hawk.' He smiled a beautiful smile.

Segun told him his name.

'Siddown, siddown, pardner,' the old man said. 'You're in the home of the Mighty Hawk. A drink?'

'Yes, no,' Segun said confusedly.

'I know what you mean exactly. It have some questions that only have that kind of answer, yes, no.' He brought out two tumblers and an unopened bottle of rum. Without offering Segun an alternative, he poured them both half-glasses.

Segun enjoyed his first sip of rum, appreciated its sweet warmth. On the old man's prompting, he finished telling his story.

'Yes, Ah recognised your description of her. She have a certain something, the way she sashay when she feeling good with the world, and roll her behind when she feeling a little vex, and that face proud and beautiful. Is about six months since Ah been seeing her around. Surprised to see a girl of that class in Brixton. Surprised some German or Englishman ain't snatch her up. It have some men who can do that, you know. See a woman and buy her for years, until he gets bored with her or her beauty starts to fade, like a shirt that's been washed too often. Yes, mahn, you ain't going to hold on to she too easily. You have my sympathy and Ah wish you good luck.

'Mind you, when she came Ah was already in love with Folake. She's been there for a few years now. Tell her all the time Ah'm going to marry her and take her to live in the forest in a tropical country where we'd make love night and day and breed a tribe of pickneys. Tell her that all the time.' He chuckled to himself.

Segun's eyes were drawn back to the black-and-white photograph. He asked the old man why he described his father as 'a hard act to follow'.

The Mighty Hawk poured them both a drink, saying, 'Now that is a long story . . .'

If Segun had been about sixty, and had lived in London since the Second World War, if Segun Adebayo had been an *aficionado* of calypso, he would have recognised the Mighty Hawk immediately. There was a time, long before his uncomfortable existence in a Brixton tower block, when the Mighty Hawk enjoyed a measure of fame and fortune. You may remember the Mighty Hawk from those black-and-white newsreel pictures of Caribbean immigrants landing in one or other English port. The spotless white Panama hat, matching white linen zoot suit, the unbelievably radiant smile in a dark handsome face, and him strumming his guitar and singing a sunny song about sun, sea and sky, with his breath all misty from the cold. Perhaps you remember the calypso that made him famous some years later, 'Oh England'.

> She call me from across the sea,
> Ah just couldn't say no
> Because she look so prettee
> Ah say let we go.
> Oh England, oh England.
>
> She call me into she room
> With a wink of she eye
> Ah say Ah coming back soon
> But when Ah see she prize
> Oh Gawd, oh England.

His background made him an unlikely calypso star. Christened Ignatius Augustus Smith, the Mighty Hawk was born into a prosperous and eminently respectable Trinidadian family. Joshua Smith, his father, had been head of the Trinidad Public Works Department and the most senior bureaucrat in the island's colonial civil service. His mother had had ambitions for him to become the first black Pope. Both were bitterly disappointed when he disappeared from Queen's College and resurfaced months later as Trinidad's most promising young calypsonian whose highly original compositions were enhanced by outlandish costumes.

Joshua Smith was so outraged that in his stiffest most admonitory voice he told the young Mighty Hawk that if he had respect for his family he would abandon this calypso foolishness or leave the island until he found sense. The young calypsonian took the latter option, leaving with a fierce determination to return in triumph and watch his father eat his words.

He had been living in London for some years before he wrote the calypso which made him famous – 'Oh England'. Many years after its release he and his band, The Trinidad All Stars, regularly featured on television. They spiced up drearily earnest shows with the Mighty Hawk's calypso songs, which often commented on topical issues and, regardless of the issue, always managed to sound lubricious. The lyrics of his song were incomprehensible to most of his audience. His pelvic gyrations, though, spoke a universal language. Then there were his costumes – the Mighty Hawk as a Roman gladiator, as an Arabian prince, as a medieval knight – which he designed himself and which distinguished him from the shipload of calypsonians who had sailed to Britain in search of fame and fortune.

Triumphant in Britain and several European countries, the Mighty Hawk's homecoming was none the less an unmitigated disaster. Having spent ten years performing and writing calypsos for an English audience, he was considered too mild, too stiff, not loose enough by the Trinidadians – though his costume, modelled after Columbus, elicited some applause. The Port of Spain audience pelted him with rotten mangoes and booed him off stage. Later in the same show, a local calypsonian, Attila the Fun, renowned for his extemporaneous compositions, ridiculed the Mighty Hawk in song:

> De Mighty Hawk say Trinidad too small
> So he pack he bags and go to London.
> De Mighty bird go find fame abraawd
> Now he fly home sounding like a pigeon.
> Englishman, go home, go home, Englishman
> Leave calypso to a real Trinidadian.

Unable to face his father, the Mighty Hawk fled back to London, crushed, dejected. For months he languished in the doldrums, unable to perform or write. He made a brief come-back with a single which looked as if it might reach the top one hundred in the pop charts but sunk soon after that flare of promise. That same year his father died. Since then he had survived by giving occasional performances in schools and talks on the history of carnival.

'But why did you give up?' Segun asked. 'A true artist never gives up.'

The Mighty Hawk had up until now told his story with irony, laughing at the vicissitudes of his colourful life. Suddenly he became serious. 'Who says I give up? I was taking a rest. Last year I decided that I was going to make a come-back, I going to show the world that the Mighty Hawk have an imagination like the sea; it can't done. I was going to build a cathedral to that imagination so they would all come and look with awe and respect. Even the old man would have to respect me from beyond the grave. I wanted to make a costume, something inspired, something fabulous, something fantastic. The idea of a mask came to me, then a costume to go with it. I worked on it like a mad man, night and day for over six months, with that photograph of the old man staring down at me. This time I was going to beat he rass. I premiered it at the Notting Hill Carnival last year, but those philistines didn't take any notice. So 'bout three months ago, I start wandering around in it at night. Man, I can tell you, I was noticed then, really noticed. You read *The Times* today?'

'You mean, you are the one, the one has been terrifying people? The one who Leah has been looking for?'

'I don't know any Leah, but is me, yes. Make front page of *The Times*, to rass.'

'But why, what pleasure can you get frightening people?' Segun said.

'None. I didn't make it to scare anybody. I made it to be noticed as an artist. Now that's done, I ain't got no use for it. Tomorrow I going to reveal my identity to the world.'

'And then?'

He sipped his rum and said solemnly, glancing at his father's picture: 'And then, maybe I'll go back to Trinidad. When I saw that photograph in this morning's paper, is like a huge weight lift off my shoulder, is like I freed from something. But, you know, all day I been trying to work out things on that old man and the way I seemed to spend most of my life rebelling against him but still looking for his love and respect. You know, I didn't even go to his funeral. Couldn't go home. It have many people like that in this London, you know. Exiles. Not because of politics or anything foolish like that. I mean exiles of the heart.'

The Mighty Hawk had begun to elaborate on what he meant by exiles of the heart when the sound of a door opening came from the corridor beyond the flat.

'That must be Folake,' the Mighty Hawk said.

Segun Adebayo, sluggish from the alcohol, stood and swayed a little.

'Cool it, man,' the Mighty Hawk said. 'If you go out there, this late at night, a total stranger, you'll frighten the life out of her.' He rose and walked stiffly to the door. He opened it and said good evening. Segun heard a Lagos accent return his greeting.

'There's somebody here to see you,' he said. He beckoned to Segun.

Segun pressed past the old man with eager anticipation. 'I'm looking for Sade,' he said as soon as he saw the young woman, who was dressed in a heavy blue coat and stylish brown shoes; her face proud and noble.

'Sade? I just saw her off at the airport. She's gone to New York. Who are you?'

Segun's heart sank. The words 'New York' resounded in his head like the distant roar of thunder. Silently he prayed to Yemanja for the strength to remain standing, to cross the Atlantic yet again. He would pour libation to Oshun to bear his message to the Yemanja, to Ogun, too, for the new journey ahead. He would . . .

It was the Mighty Hawk who had the presence of mind to ask if Folake had an address for Sade.

'Depends on who wants to know,' she said suspiciously.

Segun, though demoralised and dispirited, stepped into the corridor and launched into a slurred, disjointed version of his story, thinking at the same time about how he would get his fare to New York. When he had finished Folake revealed that Sade had often talked about him, her loving pauper with no fine embroidered clothes, only his dreams, his bountiful breeze pies. Talked of how they might one day come together again, when they could build a future on more than love. What else was there to build a future on? Segun thought, his heart rising again like a phoenix from the ashes. Already he could feel the guiding presence of the goddess Yemanja and her sister Oshun.

Chapter Twenty-one

The Caribbean Sunset Café had been closed for the day. Its blinds were down, but they were so buckled with age that the evening light streamed through onto the tables and chairs in broad horizontal bands.

Boswell had seated Gilbert beside the counter and brought out two tumblers and a bottle of Scotch. Over the years of their long friendship he had often seen Gilbert distraught, racked by nervousness and temporary loss of confidence. A good measure of whisky had always helped to restore his composure. Boswell himself had felt in need of such a tonic after Carmen's recent departure, to soothe the painful memories of doomed love and the many ambivalent feelings that her presence had stirred.

Unfortunately he had neither had a drink, nor spoken to Gilbert as yet. No sooner had he placed the bottle and glasses before his visitor than the telephone rang. An elusive debtor, whom he had been pursuing for days, had finally returned his call. Though eager to join Gilbert he had taken the opportunity to make a few urgent calls to chase up two other debtors. It was imperative that he mustered as much cash as he could for the game tomorrow.

With those calls out of the way, buoyed by solemn promises that those accounts would be settled in the morning, Boswell now went to join Gilbert. He was surprised to find him calmly sipping his drink, with the beatific expression of someone who had just won a small fortune on the horses. This was not the Gilbert he had seen burst through the door less than an hour ago. This was not a Gilbert suffering from an attack of nerves and in need of advice and reassurance.

'Well, it seems that all you needed was a stiff drink,

Gilbert,' Boswell said. He poured himself a drink and topped up Gilbert's glass.

'Like a camel that's just crossed the Sahara.'

'What happened? When you came in you looked like you meet that Dundus fellow.'

'I did, but that was months ago. I get over that long time. I was excited, man. I admit I ain't looking my sartorial best. Could do with a shave too. But otherwise things are great. Great, man. Better than they've been in a long, long time.'

'So, what's all this about going home?'

'That's what I'm so excited about. I was sitting on Hackney Downs. You know I sometimes go there to think. It's a good place to think. Open space. Anyway I was sitting there thinking about my life, Sushi, how much I miss her. She been away for months. How much I miss my family back home, when all of a sudden I look up, and I look north and saw those concrete tower blocks. I looked west and saw the redbrick estates. Like I was seeing them for the first time. Everywhere I looked I saw buildings upon ugly buildings that seemed to me like prison walls. And I remember the banana plantation where I was born, and I said to myself, man: Gilbert, this London is hell of a city. Is perdition. Is punishment. And is a punishment I inflict on myself. And for what? A wrong I did almost thirty years ago? Even murderers ain't punished for so long. So I just decided there and then to end this sentence. I decided that I'm going home.'

Gilbert's confident, almost triumphant announcement sent a tremor of discomfort through Boswell, which he disguised by lighting a cigarette.

Ever since that afternoon, many years ago, when Gilbert brought tears to the eyes of the Caribbean Sunset Café customers who heard his story, Boswell had had a deep and special affection for his compatriot. Boswell knew of no other person who shared his exile so completely. There had been numerous occasions when he had felt so close to Gilbert. So close that he had almost invited Gilbert into that most private chamber of his life where his secret lay. So close that he had almost revealed to Gilbert that they had far more in common than frozen memories of a picturesque island and a fondness for Scotch. But the masquerader in him had always enabled him to exercise self-censorship at the last moment. This ability had given him a sense of power, of superiority over Gilbert, which had been reinforced each time Gilbert sought his help. But the Gilbert who sat before him was not in need of Boswell's platitudes and sympathy. Somehow, from somewhere, he had found the strength to end his exile. He's become like all the others, Boswell thought bitterly, like those fellows at Bobby Summers' farewell party with their talk of death and departure.

'That's what you disturb my afternoon to come and tell me?' Boswell said, unaware of the injured tone in his voice.

'Bosy, it was like – like Moses before the burning bush when I realise I didn't have to be here, man. Like some kind of knowing handed down from above. I had to tell somebody. I'd have gone home and told Sushi if she had been there. Way I see it, if God spare I've got another ten, fifteen years left to me. Better that I go home. Pass it there. Me and Sushi. Maybe you could recommend a shipping agent, though. It ain't that we have plenty of things. So what you think?'

'Doesn't seem like you need my advice.'

'That's true. My mind's made up. But you don't think it's great thing?'

'I don't know, Gilbert. Somebody once said a man who's tired of London is a man who's tired of life.' Boswell laughed sourly.

'London's been my prison, Bosy. And I'm tired of this prison. I've seen babies grow up and become men and women here. Maybe for them, those born here, those who didn't come here with all our, our emotional baggage, London's different. A great place. Maybe. But I've never known that London.'

'And what you expect to find at home? A paradise? Remember how I used to talk about sitting in the sea and watching the clouds weep in the mountains? Well, I hear you can't see the mountains for the car exhaust fumes, and you can't sit in the sea for the pollution. But you're probably planning on going back to your people's farm. Country people have a long memory, Gilbert. Do you think they will have forgotten or forgiven you?'

'Things will have changed at home. I expect that. Is not a museum. Only for those of us who left it's a museum. Something fixed. Unchangeable. I'll go home, man. See if I can find a space there for myself.'

'A space to die,' Boswell said, with thinly veiled contempt.

'If you put it like that. But maybe I'll find life, too. Long ago I heard that Victoria had a son, our son. Maybe I can find him. I'll have a lot of explaining to do. But I feel I'm up to it.'

Boswell stood up and with his eyes trained to the floor, walked to the café's entrance and back. He felt both bitter and malevolent; felt a cruel desire to wound his friend. He picked up his drink and said calmly, 'Seems like you've really given the whole thing some serious thought. You have all the answers. But tell me this, Gilbert, tell me before you go sailing off to your Caribbean sunset: What happened between you and Mona?'

'Nothing,' Gilbert said, reaching for his glass.

'How d'you mean, nothing? She was in your flat before she went and killed herself. Poor child.'

'I'd ordered a suit from her father. She brought it round. When she left she seemed perfectly alright.'

'Then why you been behaving kind of strange lately? Haven't seen you in here for ages, not since that poor child died, as if you have something to hide. Now you come in here telling me you're going home.'

'I had a lot on my mind, man. Was trying to work things out. I mean, is a shame about Mona, a real shame. But from what I've heard, her family has a lot to answer for.'

Boswell rested his glass on the counter, then glared at Gilbert and said: 'You know something, Gilbert. I think you're lying. Something happened between you and that child. Now you want to run away.'

Gilbert did not appear to be intimidated. He said: 'Why

you insist on calling her a child, Bosy? She was a woman.'

Boswell, feeling a sudden urge to strike Gilbert, struggled to contain himself. He took another sip of Scotch. 'Huh, a woman? You didn't see something was wrong with her. She was a child.'

'She was a bit slow-witted, that's all. But she wasn't a child. And don't say you didn't notice. I saw the way you looked at her sometimes.'

All of a sudden Boswell lost control. He slammed his glass down on the counter, spilling his drink. Then he spun round, seized Gilbert by the shoulders, pulled him upright and punched him in the face. Gilbert staggered backwards, his features twisted in perplexity and shock. Boswell leapt towards him and struck him again, shouting: 'I told you not to trouble her, Gilbert. I told you.'

Gilbert fell on a table and rolled off, pulling down two chairs with him as he went. Boswell dropped on his knees, his fist raised to strike again.

'I didn't do anything that she didn't want, Bosy. I didn't force her against her will,' Gilbert cried, wriggling free from Boswell's grasp.

'Then why you lie to me? You lying, dirty coolie,' Boswell shouted, scrambling after Gilbert. He lunged forward and found himself forcefully repulsed by Gilbert's feet.

As Boswell flew backwards, Gilbert shouted: 'The last man who called me a dirty coolie had to run for his life.' So saying Gilbert pulled a shocked and giddy Boswell up and now returned the punch he had earlier received. Boswell crashed onto a table and the sound of breaking wood echoed through the café. Gilbert now dived onto Boswell and the two men wrestled with murderous ferocity, upturning most of the tables and chairs. One minute Gilbert had the advantage, seizing Boswell's throat in a strangling grip, the next Boswell somehow managed to snap Gilbert's hold, and heave him off. Before Gilbert could recover Boswell brought a table down on him. Gilbert thrashed about confusedly trying to remove the table, which gave Boswell the advantage. He fell on Gilbert and pinned his shoulders down with his knees.

Boswell's fist was raised, ready to pummel Gilbert's face, when he suddenly realised that he was not striking Gilbert to avenge Mona. Gilbert's behaviour had been dishonourable by his, Boswell's, private morality, which was inseparable from his ambiguous feelings for Mona. But Gilbert had not committed a crime. Mona was, after all, a woman. No, he was fighting Gilbert because Gilbert was deserting him, because Gilbert had decided to join the exodus back home, because his closest friend in his long exile was abandoning him at a time when he needed somebody over whom he could feel superior, when he needed a distraction from his own crumbling private world.

He looked down on Gilbert, saw the terror in his eyes, the hurt he had caused, and found himself unable to strike. He staggered up, leaving Gilbert on the floor, shook his head violently, shook his head in a desperate attempt to restore his mask.

Gilbert remained on the floor trembling until Boswell extended a hand to help him up.

While Gilbert wiped the blood from his lips, Boswell said: 'I'm sorry, man. I don't know what came over me.'

He walked back to the table where they had been drinking. He picked up the bottle and with shaking hands refilled their glasses. He thrust a glass at Gilbert, who took it. Then Boswell walked amongst the broken tables and chairs and righted those he could. He frustratedly kicked those which refused to remain erect.

Gilbert cleared his throat and said in a hoarse voice: 'Look, Boswell, I'm sorry, man. I didn't know it would lead to that. When I heard Mona had killed herself, I was all mashed up. For days and days I was sick with guilt, like I had swallowed a serpent that was eating out my insides. It was only when I began to hear about her brothers that I started to feel less guilty. I ain't saying that their wrongs against her lessen mine . . .'

Boswell stepped over the broken furniture, placed a hand on Gilbert's shoulder and said: 'Go home. Go home to Jamaica. Go home to Sushi, man. You don't know how lucky you are to have her.' His head hung, looking into his drink, he walked away from Gilbert.

'I'll help to pay for the damage,' Gilbert said to Boswell's back.

Boswell stopped, turned towards Gilbert, glanced around the devastated interior of the Caribbean Sunset Café, then fixed him with a hard, merciless stare and said: 'The damage you've done can't be fixed by money, man. Not all the money in the world.' Boswell was not sure whether he meant Mona's death, or the death of their friendship.

Chapter Twenty-two

It was about 11 p.m. when Boswell took his seat at the green baize round table on the top floor of Stone Mason's gambling salon. He nodded in turn at Stone Mason and the three other players whose faces were already obscured by arabesque swirls of cigarette and cigar smoke which drifted below the low light over the table.

Boswell had had a frantic but successful day chasing money owed him. He was as well prepared as circumstances allowed. Mentally, he felt a curious tranquillity, as if he had climbed into the eye of the storm of his life. Nothing else mattered but this game. Beyond it lay a future that was like the sea on a moonless night. It murmured and shifted but remained invisible. Victory or defeat would illuminate it.

'Understand you been resting, Boswell. Welcome back,' T-Bone Sterling said. This huge, fleshy maroon-black Jamaican with a trace of China in his dark inscrutable eyes was the bank that Boswell and the other players hoped to break. He was no stranger to Boswell. Years ago the now legendary T-Bone Sterling was just another player, another two-bit immigrant hustler on the circuit. Since then he had built up a chain of nightclubs between Birmingham and Liverpool, following a lucrative game against a Yorkshire cloth manufacturer. Periodically T-Bone Sterling graced the lower depths of the poker world, the derelict houses and garages in the cities where he had learnt his craft, cut his teeth. There he would renew the force of his legend with marathon poker games in which he took on all comers for a week, leaving the table only for the barest necessities. He had been known to lose, too. Heavily. This vincibility made him an opponent of enduring attraction to the amateur player, who, if victorious, could add his name to the list of those who had beaten the great T-Bone Sterling.

'You and me know there ain't no rest for the wicked, T-Bone,' Boswell said, barely looking up. 'But thanks anyway,' he said gracefully.

'Only two things I know can keep a man like you away from the poker table, Bosy: love or sickness. And you don't look sick to me. Man, I hope she was worth it.' This from Percy Lewis, another player. He owned a barbershop on Stoke Newington Church Street and could give a haircut as slick as an oil spill.

'I came here to play poker, not talk about Bosy's love life,' said Randy Jones. He was the youngest in the room and had the nervous, impatient air of a youngman in a hurry to get somewhere fast though he is not sure where.

'Why you in such a rush to get your young arse whipped, boy?' T-Bone Sterling said with avuncular reproof.

The others laughed and Randy Jones shot T-Bone Sterling a hateful glance. Before he could think of a suitable retort, Stone Mason interjected, 'House rule, no rassclawt talking at the table. Is bloodclawt poker we come to play.'

Percy Lewis winced, and T-Bone Sterling said: 'Please, Stone, ease up on the swearing.'

Stone Mason apologised, then he crumpled the crisp plastic that he had just removed from the pack of cards, cut the pack and shuffled it in fluid movements. He spread the cards in a fan shape, scooped them up like a man drinking water with his hand. Then, he placed them delicately in the centre of the table, saying, 'Cut.'

With a languorous shift of hand, T-Bone Sterling cut the pack. Stone Mason picked it up, and dealt each player the first two cards. The game had begun.

Boswell lit a cigarette, T-Bone Sterling a cigar; Percy Lewis, a devout Catholic, fingered the gold crucifix hanging from his neck, and Randy Jones played with the ostentatiously large gold signet ring on his left forefinger.

Randy Jones signalled that he was out for T-Bone Sterling's blood from the first game – in which Boswell folded – by winning three hundred pounds on a pair of fives to the illustrious guest's pair of fours. Randy would win the next three games.

These early games, with their promises of big money, discouraged Boswell. He preferred a slow start, time to study his opponents, identify their subtle, unwittingly revealing, little gestures.

When he was dealt a pair of jacks, his enthusiasm was revived. He gambled on them and picked up another jack on his fourth card, giving him a triple. T-Bone and Randy folded on their fifth cards, but Percy Lewis, with a pair of aces showing to Boswell's pair of jacks, betted on. Boswell, confident that Percy did not have a third ace, betted on with affected doubt. This encouraged Percy to raise the bet. When Boswell matched it, Percy paid to see him. Gathering his neat little pile of notes, Boswell felt a quiet euphoria. He started to concentrate on the flow of the cards, and how his opponents were betting.

When Boswell next became aware of the world outside, a grey dawn had chased the night away. Percy Lewis, the barber, had long retired and Randy Jones, having lost money steadily for several games, had also lost his youthful enthusiasm and was about to drop out. Seeing his crestfallen face reminded Boswell of his early days in London when he lived the kind of life he imagined that Randy Jones lived, a life of hand-to-mouth hustling, desperate lonely days of chasing ever receding dreams. He felt glad to have reached an age of tranquillity. His sympathetic regard for Randy Jones was not unconnected to his, Boswell's, performance. Although he had started without any real ardour, capricious Fortune, who usually reserves her favours for the most ardent amongst us, had smiled on him. A chain of winning hands had placed him way ahead of T-Bone Sterling, though much of his advantage came from Percy Lewis and Randy Jones.

When Randy Jones retired, fingering his gold signet ring as if deciding whether to pawn it to the housemaster, Stone Mason called a break, and sent one of the boys who spent their nights playing pool in the basement to buy some breakfast. T-Bone Sterling was not yet ready to finish and it would have been a grave offence for Boswell to withdraw now. Not that Boswell had any such intention. Somewhere in the night the game had taken on an impetus of its own, dragging a not unwilling Boswell along, tempting him with a cornucopia of promises.

While they ate, T-Bone Sterling said to Boswell: 'It's just you and me, Bosy.' He laughed loud and long. There was a devilish arrogance in his laughter, as if he believed a match with Boswell was a preposterous idea. 'You been keeping my money warm, now I want it.'

Boswell laughed with T-Bone Sterling, whom he knew was serious. We'll see, he thought defiantly. He was feeling good, strong and more than capable of lasting the course. He ignored T-Bone Sterling's teasingly arrogant remark, refusing to betray his state of mind by engaging in banter. He asked Stone Mason to send one of his boys to tell Lorette that he would be home as soon as the game finished.

By nightfall, visible through the cracked, grimy window of the third-floor room in that house in Dalston, Boswell was the owner of a nightclub in Birmingham and a vintage Jaguar car. It seemed that T-Bone Sterling was suffering from a liquidity shortage, forcing him to bet his assets. Boswell's instincts screamed at him to gather his winnings and leave. But he could not obey. The house rules were clear: as long as the other player was willing to continue, the game went on for three days. And there were no signs that T-Bone Sterling was ready to retire. Indeed, watching him chomp on his breakfast, a bank of bagels and salmon with cream cheese and ackee and saltfish with rice, Boswell had the disquieting impression of a man who had not yet started playing.

Meanwhile, word of the game had spread to the streets. In the pubs and basement dives where lesser gamblers congregated to play snooker, poker, and throw dice, everybody talked about the titanic battle between Boswell Anderson and T-Bone Sterling. In some versions of this news, initially disseminated by Stone Mason's gang of drugs runners, T-Bone Sterling was already thumbing a lift back to Birmingham, having lost everything he owned to Boswell Anderson. In others T-Bone Sterling had decimated Boswell, leaving him only the clothes he wore; and even that he owed to the magnanimity and grace of the victor.

On the second morning of the game, Boswell owned only the vintage Jaguar car. T-Bone Sterling had clawed back some of his losses by going on the offensive. There was now a permanent but barely perceptible smile on his lips.

With the loss of the nightclub, Boswell felt that the tide had irrevocably turned. He now played to ensure that when it washed him ashore he still clung to a valuable piece of flotsam from the wreckage of what had seemed for tantalising hours like a vessel bound for glory.

For many hours the scale was finely balanced. It finally began to swing against Boswell around midnight of the third night. He completely lost concentration and decided to double the bet on a pair of sevens facing T-Bone's pair of aces. That game cost him the vintage Jaguar car, and left him feeling dangerously low in confidence, unsure of his own judgement. He missed opportunities to regain the advantage. T-Bone Sterling mercilessly exploited Boswell's timidity. Within an hour, he had retrieved all the cash he had lost to Boswell.

Now, Boswell threw caution to the wind and he decided to play boldly on a pair of kings. He aimed to build at least a triple. But his money was almost finished and his opponent, betting on a pair of jacks, had raised the stakes. With a pair of fives and kings showing, against T-Bone Sterling's pair of tens and jacks – a possible full house – Boswell went for broke. He was certain that T-Bone was bluffing. He wagered the Caribbean Sunset Café. When T-Bone Sterling revealed the third jack, which gave him victory, Boswell felt as if he had fallen into an immense, bottomless hole. In his vertiginous descent he saw visions of his former life, before he had found security in the Caribbean Sunset Café – the single rooms with their single-bar electric heaters, the nights he walked through London, holes in his shoes, his clothes scant protection against the wintry cold; the diet of chips and baked beans bought with borrowed money. A steely determination to walk away with his dignity intact prevented him from betraying this frightening vision of the past and future in his face. Never had he struggled so hard to maintain his mask.

So when T-Bone Sterling extended his hand to Boswell in a respectful and magnanimous gesture, Boswell said: 'The road still has a long way to go. I'm sure we'll meet again and next time, who knows?'

'Well, let's make sure it's a few years down the road, man, 'cause it's going to take me that long to recover. That was a hell of a game.'

The two men laughed, still shaking hands. T-Bone suddenly became serious and said: 'Look, Bosy; I ain't got no real interest in your café, man. But I remember it from way back and the spirit it had, you know. Good. Great. I'm planning on opening a nightclub in Hackney. I'll need a good manager. Somebody who can create the right atmosphere. Somebody I can trust.'

Boswell thanked him but did not commit himself. He asked for a few days to think the offer over. T-Bone Sterling gave him a month. By that time he would also have to vacate the Caribbean Sunset Café.

It was 3 a.m. when Boswell stepped out into the night. A full moon hung in the sky like a stained light bulb. He had refused Stone Mason's offer of a free cab ride home, saying he needed the exercise. As he walked along Dalston Lane, he noticed how the neighbourhood had changed. Plane trees that he used to pass daily, like old friends in their solidity, had been chopped down, uprooted. Here and there thin rowan trees struggled to rise above the stifling vandalism of the human undergrowth. Factories that once hummed with the music of labour were boarded up, mute, disconsolate. He passed the ruined temple of pink marble columns and its walled-up windows with the rough mural depicting twenty-one angels on clouds playing saxophones. He did not notice it, or that his mask had begun to slip. After Downs Park station, he decided to cut through the redbrick Second World War council estate. Here stray dogs roamed amongst the tenebrous skeletal shells of burnt-out cars, and cats scratched at black plastic bags. His mask slipped an almost imperceptible degree further.

Crossing Lower Clapton Road, he became aware of a burning sensation in his chest. With this pain came the realisation that he had lost the Caribbean Sunset Café. Then it seemed to him that he had hung on to it for far too long, allowed it to blind him to other possibilities, to other ways of being in the world. He could not now recall the last time he had served more than a handful of customers in the café, the last time the basement had entertained more than a few sorry-looking drinkers, or some curious stray youngster lured there by stories they had imbibed with their mother's milk, as if he and the ambience of the blues dance were museum pieces. Relics from a dead past, preserved by obduracy and delusion. It seemed to him that a man erred fatally when he made attachments, when he settled for the familiar and the known. Had he stood still for too long, grown too apathetic, and too tired to start afresh? No. I am free again. I can make a new start now, he thought. But this optimism came to him without genuine conviction. He felt as if he had been walking for ever. Now he just wanted to surrender to his fatigue and rest. Rest a while.

He was halfway down Clifden Road, walking beside the high wall of Homerton Hospital, which runs most of the length of that stretch of road, when approaching steps and voices brought him back to the reality of the street, and his unreached destination. He felt the air around him stir as two figures passed him, but he did not see them. His chest burning, his legs aching, his mind in a state of violent agitation, he pressed on towards home. But in front of the Church of Revelation and Redemption, his resolve weakened and he leaned against its crumbling redbrick perimeter wall. Just a minute's rest, he thought, three days of chain-smoking and living off takeaway food in a smoky room. I'm not so young any more. And he could not remember his age and this frightened him. A premonitory vision, brief and bright, of death flashed before him. Still leaning on the cold wall, he turned towards the church's façade, looking at the neon cross, which remained ablaze night and day. Suddenly the secret he had borne half his life seemed like a burden of unbearable weight and he felt an urgent need to share it with somebody, lay it down, make his peace with God, the past and his conscience. His heart was heavy and his soul was so weary, so, so very weary.

Chapter Twenty-three

He was walking down a desolate street of mean, cramped terraced houses overshadowed by white tower blocks. Eyes clouded by cataracts and glaucoma, a walking stick helped him to feel his way along, his arthritic legs throbbing with an ungodly pain. He saw his body being placed in a cardboard casket in a dishevelled room that stank of the putrefaction of death. Two men brought the casket outside where children played with noisy abandon. He saw his funeral with a sole mourner, a woman dressed in black, her face concealed.

He opened his eyes and Lorette's face hovered above him. And the air smelt of camphor and his body – or was it Lorette's body – of bay rum. He felt Lorette holding his hand, holding it with a firm tenderness.

Then he saw himself and Gilbert seated on a verandah, the sea yards away, green mountains dancing in undulating steps behind them. Mona Xavier played on the beach of golden sand. She was building around herself a sandcastle of her suffering, fortified with her tears. She worked furiously but already strange creatures – half-crab, half-man – were erupting from the sand, their eyes ablaze with a cold fire. Nearby a woman strolled with a figure wearing a fabulous cape of peacock feathers. Gilbert and Mona started fading away and he stood naked before the sea. The sea foamed and churned violently and slowly there arose from its turbulent waves the immense head of a woman whom he recognised as Cleo, and she shook with a mighty laughter as gigantic waves crashed on her dark dimpled cheeks. She tossed her head and from her hair fell not water but an unending mountain range of tower blocks separated here and there by low, flat lands, a bleak, desolate windswept place. And he shouted at Cleo, 'Is this where I must die, on the edge of the marsh, in the shadow of cockroach-infested tower blocks, in these mean streets of London? Me? And I used to sit in the sea and watch the clouds weep in the mountains.' Cleo vanished and he spun and spun, like a top, on the deserted marsh. Then he heard music, piano music at once baroque and jazzy. A disembodied female voice sang a sad song, to which he now imagined he saw a couple dancing slowly in circles, the outline of their intertwined bodies glowing a sorrowful blue. When Lorette's face appeared again, he was aware of being conscious. She still held his hand and he felt a warm tear fall on his skin.

'Oh, Boswell,' Lorette whispered, 'you've been talking in your sleep.'

Boswell's eyes opened wider. The deep weariness had passed but he felt stiff. The bedroom clock told him he had slept for almost twenty-four hours and he felt he could sleep for another week. His throat itched and he coughed, a dry, rasping cough.

Lorette left the room and returned with a glass of water. Handing it to Boswell she said: 'Boswell, we have to talk. We can't go on living like this.'

'Yes, yes. I know,' Boswell said hoarsely. He steeled himself for the worst.

'No, you don't know, Boswell. Just listen, please. It's about my former marriage, my late husband. I didn't tell you everything because I thought I'd been cured.' She rose and began pacing the room, talking to herself.

'Oscar saved my life, Boswell. Before our relationship started proper, I became depressed and tried to take my life. Everything, everything had gone so horribly wrong. I was a failed singer: I couldn't go home: couldn't face all that contempt and derision. You know our people: how Miss Stanley daughter go a foreign go mek fool of herself 'bout she can sing.

'I was broke and lonely. One night I took an overdose of sleeping pills. Oscar called on me early that morning, and when he didn't hear a reply he became suspicious. He broke the door down . . . After I recovered we were inseparable. Our first year of marriage was the happiest I'd experienced.

Our careers took off. When we were together life was blissful. Oscar could make me laugh and some evenings we'd sit at home and play duets on the piano and sing together. Jesus, how that man could make me feel alive. Then things started to go wrong. I discovered that Oscar was having an affair with a waitress at the nightclub where we were playing for a month. When I faced him down he told me she'd thrown herself at him and he was sorry; it wouldn't happen again. But it did. Again and again. And each time I threatened to leave he would beg me to stay, fall on his knees, cry; said he would die if I left him. So I stayed. Told myself I could handle it. After all, I was having a good life. And when Oscar was with me, really with me, I felt happy. Sometimes I even joked with him about being an African chief with many wives. But you know, Boswell, deep down inside I was hurting. It got so that I couldn't go on stage without a few glasses of wine and steadily progressed to gin and tonic, large measures.

'I soon came to realise that Oscar needed sex like some people need food. A sickness. Oscar screwed wherever he could – toilets, subways, cars, side streets. And he screwed whoever he could, women, men; boys, girls. Maybe I was afraid of facing the loneliness again. Maybe I foolishly thought I could cure him. Ha, ha, ha . . .'

Lorette came out of her self-mocking laughter, shaking her head. She moaned: 'God, I gave that man so much love and in return he gave me so much hurt, did me so much wrong.

'Finally when he stuck one pin too many in my heart, I tried to leave. Packed a few pieces of clothes and booked into a hotel in Bristol. I don't know how he found me. But he did. In my room overlooking the river, he abased himself. When he saw that I was unmoved, he told me, with a chilling, angry voice, that I "belonged to him because he'd saved my life". That was when I saw how sick this man was; how sick I was too. For even as I was refusing him, I knew I still loved that man. That was the last time I saw him – alive. Three months later he was dead. A car crash; a dead girl, too. They'd been drinking.

'I'd moved back to London by then. Lived in a cramped

bedsit in Kentish Town. Took whatever work I could get. And in my own time worked on trying to change myself. Invent a whole new person. The news of Oscar's death was a devastating blow. But I soldiered on. I came from a big family, Boswell. Coming to London, I discovered loneliness. Got so lonely sometimes I thought I was losing my mind. And maybe I did. I started missing Oscar. You know what it is to miss somebody, Boswell? Really miss somebody you love? Every little upset and I'd burst into tears.

'Then one afternoon I started to imagine that Oscar was with me, lying beside me on my single bed, the way we used to in the early days when we were broke and we lived off boiled cabbage and cornmeal pudding. And I found it worked. The loneliness went away and for weeks I lived in and with my memory of Oscar. He was as real to me as you are.

'At some point I realised with horror what I was doing and started fighting back. By dropping out of the music circles that Oscar and I knew, I'd lost all my friends. So I began making a new circle of friends. After a while I found a man friend, Horace. We lasted for six months, then for some reason, he just disappeared one day. Didn't say a word. I thought I was cursed; I suffered from a relapse. Wasted months of my life in the company of Oscar's ghost. Not the sick Oscar, but the person I'd first met. Again I fought my way out of that blues. Three years passed, and I was a new person. And one night you walked into my life and I knew immediately that I wanted you. But sometimes you're not with me, Boswell. Not really with me. Like the last few months . . .' Lorette's voice trailed off and she started sobbing.

Now fully awake, and sitting upright in bed, Boswell remembered Carmen and her undying love for The Bird. How she seemed to imply that Marvin could protect her from herself. Now Lorette wanted him to protect her from her memories. For ever to love women who love others. And who would protect him from his own ghosts?

'Most times you're in that café even when you're with me,'

she sobbed. 'Did you ever wonder why I refused to join you there?'

Boswell shook his head and thought of the Caribbean Sunset Café's grimy walls and pervasive air of seediness.

'On that one visit I made there with you, the time I spent an afternoon there, I had a terrible sense of . . .' she hesitated in search of the right word, 'loss. Loss, yes. It was like a shrine to lost love. Maybe that's what I saw in you, Bosy. You're a priest of lost love, but you don't cure people, you need their heartache, you help them to keep it alive.'

Boswell felt as though someone had called his name on a crowded street. He looked at Lorette with awe because in her grief she had lighted upon a revelationary truth about him and the Caribbean Sunset Café. For twenty years he had been dispensing sympathy and advice on matters of the heart. But he himself lacked the ability to love, to love with strength, conviction and passion. He had left Jamaica in pain but the pain of Lucy King's deception had never really left him. He looked at Lorette: her reddened eyes, her mahogany-coloured cheeks stained with tears. Looked deep into those eyes and wondered if she was his last chance for true and everlasting love.

He felt an overpowering need to hold her in a gesture of gratitude for what she had shown him about herself. He stood up and walked slowly over to her. He knelt before her and clasped her waist and pressed his face against her breast. She held him in return, firm and gently. And they rocked to and fro, rocked steadily.

Lorette said: 'Baby love, I'm not seeing nobody else except that memory. You got to be strong and be with me, be with me. That'll drive him away. Be with me, be with me . . .'

Boswell rose and Lorette with him. Taking her hand, he led her to the bed, and for the first time in months, the scent of betrayed love was absent. Now there was a faint mustiness about the room, like the exudation of damp cloth slowly rotting. He undressed her and she him. She pulled him into bed, under the duvet, and they held each other tight. Boswell felt her heart beating against his chest and he followed its rhythm and pace as if he were a novice dancer taking lessons. And for a flashing instant the pulses of his own heart synchronised with Lorette's, filling Boswell with an ineffable joy. But he could not keep it alive. He shuddered and urged her to, 'Hold me closer, baby, hold me closer.' He so desperately wanted to retrieve that sensation which had slipped away. But when he felt his tears, which had dampened Lorette's hair, his anxiety passed. There would be tomorrow and after.

As they lay there in silence, Boswell thought: 'Yes, I can, we can do it. This intimacy, this touching, this loving, this will be our salvation. That's all we have now, and all we need. I will have to show her that I need her just as much, if not more, than she needs me.

Over the next week Boswell and Lorette walked daily in Victoria Park. They were a rare and unusual sight: a middle-aged Jamaican couple, holding hands as they strolled, seeking shelter from the rain beneath the bandstand, kissing there with the passion of two teenagers discovering love but without their casual brutality. On one of those strolls, he told her about Lucy King. Told her how he had been so wounded that he had left Jamaica swearing never to return. As if by leaving he could erase her from his memory, eradicate the pain caused by her duplicity. How wrong he had been to have believed that. She had haunted him ever since. Cleo had inspired the Caribbean Sunset Café, but the spirit of his first doomed love had inhabited it.

'Maybe that's what we saw in each other,' Lorette said, 'that we could exorcise the ghost of each other's past, or learn to live with them, no matter how painful, without them destroying our lives.'

The truth and wisdom of her remark impressed him deeply. He squeezed her hand, looked up to overcast sky and said: 'But you know, Lorette, it wasn't only Lucy and Cleo who haunted the café and me all those years. It was Jamaica, too. Haunts me still.'

'I know, Bosy, I know. It haunts me as well. Love for an island is the sternest passion.'

'Will you be my island?' Boswell said.

'If you'll be mine,' Lorette said, laughing lightly.

The sky spat and they sought shelter under a horse chestnut tree. Under its sprawling branches and dense dark leaves, they watched a gentle rain fall, their silence broken only by Boswell's remark that Jamaica is cheap in August.

Chapter Twenty-four

Boswell Anderson was alone in the basement of the Caribbean Sunset Café preparing for the Saturday night ahead. It would be the last Saturday night of the Caribbean Sunset Café: in two days' time he would hand the keys over to T-Bone Sterling, who had recently returned from a three-week convalescence at one of his homes in Jamaica. The new proprietor of the Caribbean Sunset Café had collapsed after that titanic battle in Stone Mason's gambling salon. If Boswell had owned a secluded villa with a view of hills and the music of the river, he too, no doubt, would have retreated there. Instead, he had had to drag himself home on that night of defeat, that night when his heart and soul conspired against him. Stealing out of the darkened streets, as if they had been stalking him for years and finally saw an opportunity to pounce. Lorette had saved him, redeemed him with her love.

He had conceived this closing-down celebration on an afternoon stroll with Lorette. It had been advertised on flyers – distributed by youngsters in the surrounding council estates – with the legend: 'The Last Blues Dance: The Caribbean Sunset Café is closing down. Come all lovers, come the broken-hearted, come the nostalgic.'

He wandered from the tiny bar, which also housed the sound system, down the length of the long narrow low-ceilinged basement. He gazed at the mural which decorated the back wall, remembering the penurious young artist who, years ago, had painted it in exchange for meals. He, Boswell, had never really liked the mural, which depicted a yellow sun partly obscured by a mountain tinted red. He had always thought that the setting sun should have been red because that was how he remembered the sunsets in the Jamaica of his youth, a flaming red sun, red like a hibiscus or poinsettia.

Nevertheless, he could not deny that the mural once had its admirers. They claimed it induced in them a bittersweet nostalgia; made you feel that you came from somewhere special before arriving in this cold godforsaken country. Looking at the mural now, he recalled someone comparing winter mornings to the daily dawn of a prisoner who knew neither what crime he had committed nor the duration of his sentence. Was it Gilbert who had said that? Yes, it must have been Gilbert, he decided, and the thought of Gilbert, his old drinking friend, filled him with melancholy. He had heard that Gilbert was having trouble persuading Sushi to return to Jamaica. He would call on him in a couple of days. After all, Boswell had decided, Gilbert was only a man – foolish, fallible, always in need of forgiveness.

A few hours later, the basement of the Caribbean Sunset Café pulsated with the sound of music, and its walls perspired once more from the dancing figures. Boswell was behind the bar, serving as both barman and DJ. Amongst the many strange faces were several familiar ones. Bobby Summers was still there. Apparently his wife had persuaded him to postpone their departure because their youngest daughter was pregnant and she felt duty-bound to stay for the birth. Carmen and her betrothed, Marvin, who was certainly no dancer, came early and would be amongst the last to leave. A minor incident which went unnoticed by most people convinced Boswell that Carmen had at last found her man. Marvin's languorously mean expression discouraged most men from asking her to dance. Boswell was one of the few brave admirers who got a dance from Carmen. But their tight slow movements to Marvin Gaye's 'Let's Get It On' brought out the worst in the singer's namesake and Carmen's lover. He started cleaning his nails with his flick knife. Fortunately, before Boswell and Carmen slipped across the boundary of propriety, slipped into their past intimacy, Boswell caught a glint of the deadly weapon, loosened his hold on his dance partner and maintained a proper distance for the remainder of the record. Several former regular customers, whom Boswell had not seen in years, approached him and expressed hearty congratulations and commiserations for his part in the poker game that had become a legend. A complete stranger tried to engage Boswell in conversation about the difficult time he was undergoing with his girlfriend. But Boswell was too busy with the bar and music to listen. For everybody Boswell spun the old favourites, music that made you feel sad and sweet, blues songs of lost love, of needing love, of betrayed love.

At about 1 a.m., the blues was interrupted by the arrival of a figure in a floor-length cape which, depending on how the light fell on it, looked like strands of gold thread, rubies or a million peacock-feather eyes. A circle was cleared for him and he spun and spun, dazzling the blues dancers with his fabulous costume. Then he removed his mask, to reveal a wrinkled face animated by a most beautiful smile, clicked his fingers and sang an a cappella version of 'Oh England', which a few old-timers recognised, prompting Boswell to dig out some calypso records. Then the walls really sweated.

Later, when this valedictory blues dance had peaked and was fading, with Earl Fatha Hines singing 'St James Infirmary', and only Carmen and Marvin danced, Boswell saw Segun Adebayo enter. He left Bobby Summers in charge of the bar and music, and he and Segun went into a corner and talked for a long time.

When he had heard the details of Segun's search for Sade, Boswell said: 'I was wrong, you know, about not allowing love to keep you here. You're a brave youngman, and I wish when I was your age, I'd had your courage.'

'But you said love had kept you here,' Segun said. 'Doesn't that take courage?'

'I didn't quite say that,' Boswell said. 'Truth is, it was the fear of love that kept me here.'

Segun looked at him with a puzzled expression.

Just then Boswell saw Lorette – who had promised to attend, but late because she couldn't stand the cigarette smoke – coming down the stairs. She wore an indigo outfit, which matched the blue light in the basement. Behind her the light in the stairwell had changed, morning had broken. He excused himself from Segun and went to meet her at the bottom of the stairs.

'Can I have this last blues dance with you, my love?' he asked.

'Yes. But be gentle. I'm feeling kind of tender tonight.'

'I am too old to be rough, baby,' he said, holding her close. And they danced slowly.

When they finished, Boswell turned on the lights and called out: 'Ladies and gentlemen, the last blues dance is over.'

Most people filed away, but, as in the old days, Boswell had to evict a few men whose appetite – for reasons which Boswell refused to listen to – for the melancholic music of the blues was insatiable.

Boswell carried out a last security check on the building alone and then joined Lorette above ground. The sun was rising over the marsh, as they headed home. The former proprietor of the Caribbean Sunset Café walked jauntily, like in the old days when the earth was moving in his direction. And as he walked, he thought of the horse he would back at Newmarket on Wednesday – King of Hearts – the long, long letter he would write Cleo, and the Sunday he would spend in bed with Lorette, worshipping in the temple of their love.